OUTTA TIME

A Novel
By
June Lundgren

Copyright 2016

Angelic
Character List

Martha- Elder Spirit Guide to Sophie
Ann- Spirit Guide in training to Sophie
Bert- Elder Spirit Guide to Nick
Helen- Spirit Guide in training to Nick
Sid- Spirit Guide in training to Nick

Table of Contents

Chapter 1...............................4
Chapter 2...............................14
Chapter 3...............................34
Chapter 4...............................41
Chapter 5...............................48
Chapter 6...............................64
Chapter 7...............................77
Chapter 8...............................85
Chapter 9...............................95
Chapter 10..............................100
Chapter 11..............................107
Chapter 12..............................115
Chapter 13..............................128
Chapter 14..............................139
Chapter 15..............................164
Chapter 16..............................172
Epilogue................................202

Chapter 1

"Someone's coming"

"I know someone's coming,"

"Boy, is he angry!"

"Hmm, yes, I can feel his anger. He's a non-believer, doesn't believe in 'all that nonsense', as he puts it."

"This isn't going to be pleasant. We should warn Sophie about him," Ann said, floating down off her perch on the roof of the small shop.

"No, I think we should just stay out of this for now," Martha said, landing gently on the large rhododendron bush adjacent to the walkway.

"Martha, you know something you're not telling me. All right, give; what is this all about?"

"Now Ann, you know you're still in training and information is given on a need to know basis, and you don't need to know, at least not right now. Just watch, it is all a part of your training. Come sit down with me," she said, patting the area next to her on the large bush. "You should be able to come into any situation and instantly know what's happening. Being aware of how your mortal is going to react to external forces is a part of the job. Once you understand what's going on, you can then give them advice, should they need it."

"What if I can't figure it out? What if I screw up?" Ann asked as she sat down next to Martha.

"That's why the training is so extensive; we know it takes time to become attuned to your mortal. We know that if you can attune yourself to a person who is not your assignment; then it will be easier for you when you get your assignment. As guardian angels and spirit guides, we must be in constant contact with our mortal's mind and emotions."

"Why do we need to be in constant contact? Why not just pop in occasionally?"

"Because if we're not with them, we can't guard them from the *others*," Martha explained.

"What do you mean by *others*?" Ann interrupted.

"The dark ones." Martha gave Ann a meaningful look.

"Uh, oh, I get it, the *others*, sorry. I guess I'm a little slow this morning," she apologized.

"We need to make contact with the other person's guides. Making contact with their Guide or Guardian is not always as easy as it sounds. Some, like me, have been doing it off and on since the beginning of time. Most of us remember what it's like to be a new guardian. There are some among us who either do not remember or refuse to remember the beginning. I was like that once, arrogant and uncaring."

"I don't believe it, you could never be like that, Martha. You're so warm and caring." Ann gasped.

"Believe me, Ann; I was just like some of the other old ones. I believed that I was better than the other heavenly angels and guardians because I was one of the first ones. Fortunately for me, God saw what was happening and sent for me. Standing before Him, I listened to His words. He said that I had been too long in His kingdom. I had forgotten how to care and what it was like to be mortal. In His infinite wisdom, he made the decision to send me back to a mortal life, a life full of pain, joy, fear and uncertainty. It was a lesson that I am not likely to forget. When I returned to Him, He asked what I had learned."

"What did you say?" Ann asked.

"I told Him I had learned that life was to be savored. Through the suffering, pain and uncertainty, there was one constant, His love. I knew even in the darkest times when my faith wavered that His love and forgiveness never did. I asked God if I could train the new guides and guardians, to make sure that they never forget what it means to be mortal."

"What did he say?" Ann asked, enthralled by the story.

"He told me that He would allow me to train them and I was to make sure they learned from my mistake. That was over five hundred years ago."

"Wow, I'm sure glad that He allowed you to become a guardian. You're a wonderful person, Martha, and I can't imagine a better teacher for new souls," she said, giving Martha an enthusiastic hug.

"Thank you, Ann," Martha said.

"You're welcome, finish your story, I want to hear the rest."

"All right, now where was I? Oh, yes, I remember. Every now and then, my work brings me in contact with some of the other old ones. If they've forgotten the lesson that I've learned, I take great pleasure in reminding them of it."

Ann grinned. "I'll just bet you do!" She laughed.

"Most of them take the hint and change their attitude. However, some refuse to change. If they refuse to change, they are sent back as I was, to a mortal existence. If they don't learn their lesson in the first lifetime, they return until they do."

"Well, I'll tell you one thing, if I ever forget, I know you'll give me a swift kick in the other end. But back to what we were talking about; how do I go about accessing my person's situation?" Ann wanted to know.

"That's where I come in; it's my job to help you learn how to enter a person's mind. Not only will you learn to read their thoughts, but also influence them. Sometimes they need a nudge in the right direction when they stray from their chosen path," Martha said.

"What do you mean by influencing them?"

"Now that's a very good question. There are two distinct levels in the mind; conscious and unconscious mind. In most people, the two levels rarely acknowledge each other. Usually, the subconscious remains in the background, quietly prodding the conscious mind into action when needed. But in someone like Sophie, who is able to communicate on our level, the unconscious mind plays a much greater role."

"I'm not sure I understand what you mean. Can you give me an example?"

"In the subconscious are stored the memories from the past, such as early memories and traumas that the conscious mind finds too painful to remember. An example of this is a near drowning as an infant, which the conscious mind buries in the subconscious. The person may not remember the actual incident. They only know that they have an irrational fear of drowning. This level also holds the key which unlocks past lives," Martha explained.

"I understand now, the conscious mind forgets the bad experience by relegating it to the subconscious mind. That way, the conscious mind does not have to deal with the trauma. At least not until something happens to trigger the memory. I didn't know the subconscious also held the knowledge from past lives. So how is that different for people like Sophie?" Ann asked.

"Sophie has the ability to access the memories of those past lives with the use of meditation. We'll talk more about this later, here comes trouble," Martha said, nodding at the black four by four pickup pulling up in front of the shop.

They watched as the dark haired man climbed out of the vehicle. Walking around the front, he paused on the sidewalk, seemingly admiring the crystals filling the display window.

"You wouldn't know by looking at him he's upset," Ann murmured to Martha. "I'll bet if you could see his eyes, you'd know he was angry. I wish he'd take off those sunglasses so that I can get a good look at him. I wonder what he's so angry about and why he's coming to see Sophie," Ann mused.

"Patience Ann, can you see his guides?" Martha asked.

"Yes, I don't recognize any of them. Can't you see them?" Ann asked curiously

"Yes, I can see them, but I wasn't sure if you were able to. It is not always as easy as it sounds to deal with other people's guides. Sometimes they refuse to show themselves. How many do you see?"

"There are three of them, two men and an older woman. The woman looks quite frustrated, but the other two seem to be sharing some private joke. I wonder what's so funny. I think I'll just wander over there and see what's going on," Ann said.

Reacting quickly, Martha grabbed Ann's arm. "Oh, no you don't, not so fast. Do not forget, you are still in training. Remember, it is up to the senior guardian to initiate contact with other guides. You're supposed to be observing and learning, not interfering," she admonished.

"Sorry, Martha, I just kind of got carried away." She sighed. "Michael said I'm too impulsive, that I need to learn to control my actions. I'll try to do better, honestly I will," Ann said earnestly.

Martha smiled knowingly; she would bet real money that Ann would not be able to keep out of trouble for long. She watched as the man's guardians moved toward her. She recognized one of the male figures; he was one of the few old ones who never forgot his humanity. She did not know the other two, assuming that they were newer souls.

"Martha, how are you? Haven't seen you in a few hundred years," the older of the two men greeted her.

"Bert, it's good to see you again. Still training the newer souls, I see."

"Well, it's a living, if you'll pardon the pun," he said, laughing.

"I know exactly what you mean. This is Ann," she said, drawing her forward. "She's a new guardian, still in training."

"It's good to meet you, Ann. I'll tell you right now, Martha is the best there is. You couldn't have asked for a better teacher." He motioned for his companions to join them. "This is Sid and Helen; they're guides in training. Sid, Helen, I would like you to meet someone very special, she and I go back a long way," he said, smiling at Martha. "This is Martha," he said, placing an arm around her shoulder, "and Ann is her guardian in training."

"It's nice to meet both of you, but can we get on with the subject at hand?" Helen asked.

"The subject at hand being that guy right over there," Sid said, gesturing over his shoulder to where the angry man stood. "By the way, girls, lovely to meet you," he said with a thick cockney accent, wiggling his eyebrows.

Sighing, Bert turned to where Helen stood waiting impatiently for him. "You've been doing this for nearly fifty years. Haven't you learned yet that you can't rush fate?" Shaking his head, he glanced over at Sid, only to find him distracted by Ann. "Sid, I'm sure Ann doesn't need you ogling her."

"Sorry, mate" he said, not looking in the least bit sorry.

"Maybe we should get to the matter at hand," Martha said with a knowing smile at Bert.

"Yes, well the angry young man you see before you is Nicholas Stavros. He is forty, single, owns his own business and is as arrogant as they come. He has a younger brother named Matthew and a loving mother named Jewel. His mother is a wonderful woman full of faith but also very sad, and therein lies the problem." He sighed.

"What's that got to do with Sophie?" Ann interrupted. "I know Jewel has been here to see Sophie several times. She always leaves here feeling so happy and full of hope. Sophie would never hurt anyone; in fact, she helps a lot of people," Ann said indignantly.

"Ann, remember what we talked about earlier, Michael would not be pleased," Martha warned.

"Sorry," Ann said, looking embarrassed.

"Ran afoul of Michael, did she? Well, she won't be the first or the last one to do that," Bert said, giving Martha a knowing look. Turning his attention to Ann, he said, "Calm down, little one, I know Sophie is a good person and would never hurt anyone intentionally." He glanced in Sid's direction to find him staring at Ann. "Sid, stop ogling Ann and tell her what's going on."

Grinning at Bert, he turned back to Ann. "Well, it's like this, love, Nick's father crossed over last Christmas and his mum has been inconsolable ever since."

"Sid, you idiot," Helen said in frustration, "tell them the whole story! What Sid forgot to tell you is that Jewel fell into a deep depression. She wouldn't leave the house or see any of her friends," she said, pacing in agitation. "You don't know how hard it was for me to get her to leave her bed, let alone leave the house. I worked on her for weeks to get her to accept a lunch invitation from one of her dearest friends. When Nick found out she had accepted the invitation, he wouldn't let her cancel it. She tried to back out at the last minute, but he knew it would do her good to get out. She met Jean for lunch and realized just how much she missed her friends. Jean could see how depressed Jewel had become."

"When Jewel asked Jean about her sister, she hesitated at first, not knowing how she would react to the news of her sister's death. She worried that the news would send Jewel into an even deeper depression. At Jewel's urging, Jean told her about her sister's unexpected death. She mentioned how Sophie helped her come to terms with her sister's death. Jean urged Jewel to come with her and meet Sophie. She was reluctant at first, and then agreed to meet Jean for tea the following week and visit Sophie's shop." Helen smiled serenely.

"Get on with it, will you, love? I'm not getting any younger," Sid whined.

Ann choked, trying not to laugh openly. She could see Martha and Bert were also having a hard time keeping a straight face. Sid, on the other hand, was grinning from ear to ear.

Helen shot him a withering look and continued her story. "As I was saying before I was so rudely interrupted. Jewel and Jean made a reservation for tea the following week. After tea, Jewel followed Jean to Sophie's old Victorian shop. Jewel was enchanted with Sophie's little shop and her quiet manner. Sophie was able to communicate with Jewel's husband and in doing so put her mind to rest."

"I remember her now, short, thin, frail looking woman with dark red hair," Ann interjected. "She has a beautiful soul."

"Ann," Martha warned.

"Sorry," Ann said, smiling.

Helen turned to Martha. "No, she's absolutely right, Jewel does have a beautiful soul. As you know, she has been seeing Sophie weekly over the last three months. Everything was going smoothly until Nick found out. He thinks that Sophie is a con artist, trying to get money from his mother."

"Well, I can tell you Sophie is the real thing, she's not a fake!" Ann said indignantly.

"Ann!" Martha warned.

"It's all right, Martha, I'm glad she has the gumption to speak her mind. At least we know she'll stand up for her mortal, unlike some others we know," Bert said, exchanging a secretive look with Martha.

He was remembering a time long ago when he first became a guardian. Like Ann, he was full of enthusiasm and out to show what a good job he could do. His mortal had done something that he needed to be reprimanded for, although it was for a good cause. Instead of standing up for his mortal, he had simply done nothing. He had been too afraid and unsure of his new role as a guardian to stand up in his defense. His mortal had paid the price because he did not have the backbone to stand up for him.

"What's that all about?" Ann asked Sid softly.

"Don't know, love, but it looks right interesting, it does," Sid replied, winking at her.

"So Nick's come to find out just what kind of a crook Sophie is," Bert said, grinning at Martha. "Boy, is he in for a shock. I'm just gonna sit back and watch the fur fly, I suggest you do the same."

Chapter 2

Monday morning dawned bright and sunny. Nick pulled his truck up in front of an old Victorian style cottage nestled among the larger more modern buildings. The morning summer sun bathed the cottage in its golden glow. The cottage was surrounded by a tall white picket fence. He frowned remembering his earlier conversation with his brother.

"Matt, have you noticed the change in Mom lately? A couple of months ago I couldn't even get her out of her bedroom, let alone the house, and now she's never home."

"Well, what are you complaining about? Isn't that what you were trying to do, get her out of the house to visit her friends?" Matt asked, puzzled but weary.

"Well, yes, but it's happened in such a short time, it makes me wonder how it happened," he murmured, more to himself than his brother. "It all seems to coincide with that first lunch appointment with Jane. Maybe I need to give Jane a call today and see if she has any idea."

"Damn," Matt said, "why do you have to analyze everything to death? Why can't you just be happy that Mom's feeling better?"

"I am glad she's feeling better, I'm just wondering what brought about this sudden change. Have you spoken with Mom to find out what's going on?"

"That's what I've been trying to tell you, only you won't shut up long enough to listen," Matt commented sarcastically. "I don't know, Mom wouldn't tell me, told me it was none of my business."

"Maybe I should call Jane and see what I can find out from her," he murmured to himself.

"I already talked to Jane, and she wouldn't tell me anything either. Said if Mom wanted me to know, she'd tell me."

"Well, I'm going to make her tell me what she's been up to. I only hope to God it's not some old con man trying to get money out of her," he said, starting for the door.

"Now hold on a minute, Nick. I talked to Mom again and found out what she's been up to."

"Why didn't you say something before this?"

"Because I couldn't get a word in edgewise. You were too busy giving me the third degree!"

"Well, come on out with it."

"She's been seeing a medium."

"You're kidding, right?

"Nick, what harm can it do?" Matt tried to reason with him. "Mom seems to have a new lease on life. Isn't that what we were trying to accomplish by getting her out of the house?" Nick looked disbelievingly at his brother. Matt held up his hands in a defensive gesture.

Walking over to the wet bar, Nick poured himself a beer.

"I do not want my mother duped by some phony psychic who preys on the grief of others," Nick fumed, pacing angrily.

"I know, I know, you could have knocked me over with a feather when she told me what she's been doing."

"Did you ask her how much money she's paid this phony fortune teller?" Nick asked.

"You know, I did start to question her about how much someone like this charges for something like that, and she was actually very short with me. I didn't know she had it in her." He grinned at his brother. "You know something, big brother, I kind of like the new Mom." Placing his hands on his hips, he looked at his brother and said very seriously, "I think you should just trust her on this. She is not some senile old woman, you know. She has more brains than most of the women you date," he paused for a moment, "but that's not saying much, now is it?" Grinning, he strolled over to the wine colored chaise lounge and flopped down on it.

Settling in the large grey overstuffed chair, Nick attempted to regain control of his temper. "I know she's not senile, I'm not insinuating that there's anything wrong with her mind. She is one of the most intelligent women I know. However, you must admit, where our father is concerned, her grief is impairing her judgment. Can you honestly say that you've ever known our mother to go to a psychic?" Nick asked, crossing one elegantly shod leg over the other.

"Go to one, no, believe in them, yes," Matt said, smiling knowingly at him.

"And just what do you mean by that?" Nick asked impatiently.

"You remember Mom talking about her great grandmother, Helen?" Matt waited expectantly, leaning forward in excitement.

Nick looked inquiringly at his brother.

"You don't remember, do you? I guess I shouldn't be surprised, though, you were never interested in family history." Sitting back, he made himself comfortable. "I remember Mom telling me about her great grandmother who was a rather gifted psychic. Mom has always believed she has some psychic abilities herself."

"What are you grinning at, idiot? Why haven't you said anything before now?" Nick asked angrily.

Matt held up his hand, ticking off points using his fingers. "One: you never asked. Two: you were too busy freaking out to listen. Three: you wouldn't have believed me even if I had told you."

"I still don't believe you. Mom has never said anything to me about having psychic abilities," he growled in frustration.

"Do you remember when Mom told you not to go on that fishing trip last year? You thought it was because she didn't like Laura. Sure, she didn't like her, but then none of us did." Matt stood up, walking over to the bar, he poured himself a soda. Turning to face his brother, he said, "It was because she had a feeling that something bad was going to happen to you, and it did. She tried to warn you, but you blew her off, like you always do."

"I did not blow her off; I just thought she was being overly worried about nothing," Nick said reflectively. "How was I supposed to know we would get stranded at sea for three days?"

Matt gave him a speculative look, *wondering not for the first time how his brother could be so closed-minded.* Taking a long drink of his soda, he returned to his seat.

"What do you know about this, so-called, psychic?" Nick asked.

Matt groaned inwardly, *this was not going to be pretty. He felt sorry for the unknown psychic.* "I don't know much, Mom wasn't exactly forthcoming. The only thing I know is that it's a woman and she works out of a crystal shop in the Sellwood district."

"It may take me a few days, but I'll find her, you can be sure of that," Nick said, looking stonily at Matt. Placing his glass on the counter with exaggerated care, he turned and left the room.

Nick was startled abruptly back to the present by a loud noise close by. He turned to find a garbage truck pulling around the corner. Glancing at his watch, he realized that he had been standing on the sidewalk for several minutes. Turning back to the small shop, his anger rekindled at the thought of the phony psychic who had preyed upon his mother's grief. He smiled to himself, relishing the idea of putting the fear of God into this woman. *She would never prey on another grieving person after today.* He started towards the shop door but was momentarily distracted by a flash of something out of the corner of his eye.

Stopping, he looked to his left to see what had caused the flash. He couldn't see anything that might have caused the sudden flash of light. Looking back at the shop, for the first time he noticed the sign above the door, it read 'Outta Time Crystals'. He noticed the cottage had an octagonal torrent, which was unusual. They usually put round torrents in the design of Victorian era cottages.

Glancing at the door, he noticed a small crystal wind chime hanging over it. *That must have been what caused the flash of light,* he thought. Shrugging his shoulders, he continued up the stone path to the door. Reaching for the doorknob, he turned it, but nothing happened. He looked at the sign on the door that indicated hours of operation. To all intents, the shop was open, he tried the knob again. When that didn't work, he knocked loudly on the door. He listened for a moment or two and heard the faint sound of footsteps growing louder the closer they got to the door.

"I told you it wouldn't work, but did you listen?" Helen said, glaring at Sid. "Why doesn't Nick ever listen to us?" she asked, looking up towards heaven. "I know he's stubborn, but I also know he could hear us if he really wanted to." Turning to Bert, she gave him a look of pure frustration. Walking over to where Nick stood, she gave him a kick in the seat of his pants. He didn't even flinch.

Turning, she headed back to where the others were waiting. They stood unmoving, staring at her as if unable to believe their eyes. She gestured to where Nick stood waiting at the door. "Did you see that? He didn't even feel it," she shouted in angry frustration, waving a fist at him.

Suddenly, the spell that held the other guardians immobile broke. They started to laugh, the more Helen glared at them, the harder they laughed. Stomping her foot in anger, she shouted at them, "It's all very well for you to laugh; you're not the one trying to get through to that pigheaded idiot."

The laughter grew louder, and suddenly Helen found herself was joining in. She could not believe she actually had the nerve to give Nick a swift kick in the seat of his pants.

"Helen, you are delightful," Martha said, smiling at her and giving her a quick hug.

"Way to go, Helen, too bad he couldn't feel it. You have to work on that, love. With a bit more energy behind you, you could have made him feel it! Shall I give it a try, love?" Sid asked eagerly.

"Sid," Bert said warningly, "this is not the time for that." Looking at Martha, he raised an eyebrow in question. "What do you suggest we do about our little dilemma?"

"I think we should sit this one out," Martha advised.

"Are you out of your mind?" Helen all but shouted.

Martha and Bert glanced inquiringly at her. "I've never seen him so mad. What if he blows up at Sophie? I know he would never physically hurt her, but if you'll pardon the expression, he could sure scare the hell out of her."

"I vote we go in there and make sure he doesn't hurt Sophie," Ann said, looking at Sid.

"I'm with ya, love, let's do it," Sid said, grabbing Ann's arm. They headed arm in arm for the shop.

Nodding his head, Bert threw up an invisible wall in front of the two wayward guardians. They ran right into it, bouncing off it and landing on the ground.

"Hey, who did that?" Ann asked, looking over her shoulder, her eyes met Bert's. "That's not fair, we were only going to make sure that Sophie was safe."

"You were interfering, and that I will not allow," Bert said. "Ann is new, and I can excuse her, but you should know better than that, Sid."

"Sorry, I sort of got carried away, won't happen again," he said, grinning. Noticing the look in Bert's eyes, Sid held up his hands in self-defense. "Okay, okay, I'll behave, I promise." Looking at Ann, he grinned. "We had better behave, or we'll both end up in limbo. Take my word for it, that is one place you do not want to be," he said, his face serious.

"Ann, I think we need to let Sophie handle this on her own. She may look fragile, but don't let her looks fool you," Martha said with a knowing smile. "She has the heart of a lion and the stubbornness of a mule. She'll give as good as she gets."

"Well, that's settled then." Sid jumped to his feet and held out his hand to help Ann up. "I don't know about you guys," Sid said, grinning at Ann, "but I'd sure like to be there when these two get together."

Grabbing Ann's hand, he started toward the house.

"Sid, I think you need to butt out," Helen said, crossing her arms and setting her jaw.

"But they won't even know we're there, it'll be fun," Sid cajoled.

Ann removed her hand from Sid's clasp. "Sid, Sophie can hear us, she knows when we're there," Ann informed Sid softly.

"Well, she may be tuned into you, but she can't hear me. I'll just sit quietly and not say a thing," Sid said earnestly.

Bert, who had been silent through the entire exchange, spoke up. "Sid, Sophie has been gifted by God. You do remember what that means, don't you?

Ah," Bert smiled at Sid, "I see by the look of surprise on your face that you do remember."

"Hello," Helen interrupted, tapping her foot impatiently, "hello, are we going to intercede or not? I for one would like to be present when they meet." She looked at Bert a twinkle in her eye. "Isn't it true that old ones can hide themselves from even those who are gifted?" she asked, looking at Martha for confirmation.

"Yes, it's true. There is a way to keep mortals from seeing and hearing us." Martha shrugged. "We don't often have to go to such lengths to hide ourselves. Normally, they feel us in one way or another because of our connection. I am hoping with Nick as a distraction, she won't give it more than a passing thought." She looked at Sid, Ann and Helen. "You three will have to be extremely quiet, or you'll have to remain here," she warned sternly.

"I promise to be quiet, Martha, honestly I will," Ann promised, looking earnestly at Martha and Bert.

"I can hold my tongue, but," Helen said, looking pointedly at Sid, "I'm not sure about lover boy over there."

"Hey, what did I do? I can be quiet when the need arises, luv," Sid protested. "I promise on my honor to keep quiet. If I don't, you can banish me to limbo."

Bert smiled wickedly at Sid. "You can be sure of that. Oh, by the way, I will be grading you on how you do in this type of a situation. A lot will depend on your self-control. If you fail this test, well, let's just say it won't be pleasant."

"What will happen if I fail the test?" Sid looked worriedly from Bert to Martha.

"Well, let's just say it will mean starting over," Bert said soberly. "Martha, are you ready?"

"Yes, you can release the door now." She smiled at Bert.

Nick heard the footsteps stop on the other side of the door. He could hear someone rattling the handle from the other side.

"It seems to be stuck, try turning the handle and giving it a push," a soft voice instructed from the other side of the door.

"Okay, stand back, I'm going to give it a shove," Nick shouted. Taking a step back, he threw his weight against the door.

It was unfortunate that Bert choose that precise moment to release his hold on the door. Nick landed with a thud on the floor at Sophie's feet.

Grinning, Sophie looked down at the man lying at her feet. "Well, that's one way to make an entrance." Resting her hands on her hips, she asked, "Are you going to get up, or do you enjoy lying on the floor?"

Looking up, Nick encountered a pair of thick-fringed golden eyes staring down at him. He had the uncomfortable feeling that they could see into his soul. "I usually walk in on my own two feet," he said, getting to his feet and straightening his clothes. "You need to have that door checked."

Cocking her head to the side, she gave him a considering look. "It's never stuck before, I wonder…." She trailed off, lost in thought.

Closing the door, Nick turned to find one of the largest pit bulls he'd ever seen standing next to the woman with the strange eyes. The dog came up beside her, bumping against her leg. She reached down and stroked its head. It stood, by his estimation, about three and a half feet tall to the top of its head. The look in its eyes said not to come too close, as he was still reserving judgement about him.

"Ugh, that is one of the biggest pit bulls I've ever seen," he said.

"Yes, he is quite large. He started out being the runt of the litter, and the owner was going to have him put down. I asked if I could have him instead, and look how beautifully he turned out. I told him he needed to grow tall and be proud, and he did."

"Well, he certainly listened."

"Yes, he's my guard dog, we take care of each other," she said, reaching down to nuzzle his head.

Taking advantage of her preoccupation, he studied her intently. She looked to be around twenty-five, with long, dark chestnut hair. She was dressed in some kind of flowing top and a pair of figure hugging jeans. *Her figure was a little rounder than he liked in a woman, but he could not deny he found her attractive.*

"What's his name?"

"JT."

"Does it stand for something, or is it just initials?"

"It stands for just trouble. When he was a pup, he always seemed to get into some kind of trouble," she said, laughing.

Silence, nothing but silence, Sophie sighed inwardly. She couldn't feel her guides, and the silence was almost deafening. It was not unusual for them to fade into the background to give her some personal space. However, she usually felt their presence even through the silence. She could neither hear them nor feel their presence. *Something was definitely up, that door had never stuck before. She was sure it was not just a coincidence that Mister Good Looking here was at her door. She could feel the anger emanating from him, and his aura was pulsing with varying shades of red, green and yellow.*

She could feel his eyes moving over her, taking in her appearance and finding her wanting. She heaved a sigh of resignation and figured that she had better see what this was all about.

"I'm sorry about the door; I'll have my handyman check it. You're not hurt, are you?"

"No, I'm not hurt; just my pride, that's all."

"Now that you've made it inside, how can I help you?"

Now that he was inside, *he needed to find out if she was the so-called psychic. He needed to have a good reason to be in the shop first.* He tried to think up an excuse. Just then, his eye was caught by a flash of color. "I was told that you have quite a collection of crystals. I'm looking for something unusual for a birthday present. The person I'm buying for collects unusual crystals," Nick explained.

Sophie felt sure he was not being completely honest with her. She had the feeling that the birthday present was a convenient excuse for something much deeper.

All right, she thought, *I'll play along, let's see where it leads.*

"I have several beautiful pieces over here," Sophie said, leading him over to a window display.

Nick glanced at the display, then back at Sophie. "These are beautiful, but they're not what I'm looking for. Don't you have any special pieces? Something you don't keep on display?"

She gave him a considering look, then turned and headed towards the back of the shop.

Nick watched as she weaved her way around the displays and disappeared towards the back of the shop. He followed her; once there, he noticed a small ornate filigree-covered door. He assumed that it led to a storage area. To the left of that, he found a secluded alcove with a small table and two wing chairs. Taking a quick look around in the alcove, he noticed that it was almost empty. A large crystal pyramid sat in the middle of the table, candles glowed softly on the shelves that lined the circular area. There seemed to be something unusual everywhere you looked.

"I thought all fortune tellers used crystal balls," he muttered to himself.

"Do you believe everything you see on TV? The only fortune tellers you'll find are in the movies," Sophie replied sarcastically. He hadn't heard her come up behind him and had not realized that he had spoken aloud.

"Crystals are used to focus psychic energy, not tell fortunes. Although, some people use them for scrying. If you'll come over here, I have something unusual that you might be interested in." Turning, she headed for the front of the store, leaving him to follow.

Following her, Nick noticed how the flowing top she wore hugged her figure to perfection. He was unaccustomed to finding himself drawn to a woman against his will. After all, she was a cheat and a liar, preying on the weakness of other people's grief. Giving himself a mental shake, he followed her into a large, spacious room just off the main shop. "What is scrying?" he asked.

She looked at him, raising an eyebrow in question. "Do you really want to know, or are you just asking?"

"I really want to know."

"Scrying is a form of looking into the future. People use things like mirrors, a thin bowl of water, a black plate, candle flames and even a crystal ball to see the future. The person wanting to see the future clears their mind and gazes into the reflective surface. If they have the ability, they will see the future events in the reflective surface. This form of telling the future goes back to the time of Nostradamus."

She raised her eyebrows at him and questioned, "You've heard of Nostradamus, right?" Sighing, she muttered under her breath, "Well, never mind; I should have known you wouldn't know who I was talking about."

The first thing he noticed about the room was its unusual octagonal shape. The walls were made of glass, except where it met the rest of the house. The ceiling was open beam, and between the beams were stained glass panels. The panels were filled with images depicting the creation of the universe. The floors looked to be oak inlayed with images of angels. The overall effect was one of openness and light. The room was almost devoid of furniture, except for two pieces. A single chair and octagonal glass table stood as the centerpiece of the room. Several large, round pillows were placed along the outside perimeter of the Room. He wondered what she used this room for.

"This room has the most direct light; therefore, it's perfect to view crystals."

He moved over to where she stood at the table. She placed a large wooden box on the table and opened it. Impatiently, he waited to see what the box contained.

"This is a piece that is one of a kind; it was created by a friend of mine that specializes in unusual crystal sculptures," Sophie said as she carefully lifted the cloth covered crystal statue out of the box and placed it on the table.

Nick waited while she removed the cloth-encased object and placed it in the center of the table. At that precise moment, a ray of sunlight reflected through the crystalline statue, nearly blinding him. He could almost swear that he had seen the statue move, but of course, that was just an optical illusion he told himself. Rubbing his eyes, he tried to clear his vision. As his vision cleared, he stared at the object, which sat in the middle of the table. He sat down in the chair next to him and stared at the crystalline figure. He had never seen anything like it. It was a cluster of four different objects linked together by a fine thread of crystal. The bottom was an angelic figure with arms stretched up towards heaven. In the right hand the angel balanced a figure of the sun. And in the left hand she balanced a figure of the moon. Connecting the moon and sun was an intricate star. Each object looked like it was suspended in mid-air.

"I've never seen anything like it," Nick commented. "The celestial objects look like they are floating in mid-air."

"Yes, the artist is very talented, she is a local artist. What's even more remarkable is that she's blind."

Nick shot her a look of pure astonishment. "You're kidding, right? I would have to see it to believe it. If she is blind, how can she possibly create something that detailed? I know sighted artists that aren't that good."

"She has an extremely sensitive sense of touch, as all Indigo children do. She also has the ability to *see* using her third eye. Few people are able to do that to her extent."

Nick raised an eyebrow in inquiry. "What are Indigo children, and what is a third eye?" he asked.

She looked intently into his unusual grey eyes, trying to determine if he was seriously interested or just giving lip service. "Do you really want to know, or are you just humoring me?"

Nick surprised himself by answering, "I really want to know."

Pausing for a moment, she explained, "Indigo children are children born in the last thirty years who have been born with special abilities. These abilities range from the ability to see the future, speak with those who have died, as well as angels. No matter what ability they have, all these children have some form of heightened senses, such as hearing, vision, taste or touch. The third eye is a spot located in the center of the forehead. It is a connection between the physical world and the other side. Everyone has the ability to open his or her third eye, but most choose not to. I have found the reason most choose not to open this doorway is that they are afraid of what they will see. They also fear losing control of themselves.

What they don't realize is that control is just an illusion," she said, looking meaningfully at him.

"Yes, well everyone is entitled to their own opinion, and I for one believe I'm in control of my own destiny."

"I agree, everyone has a right to their own opinion, and I do not force my beliefs on other people. I respect other people's opinions, and I expect them to respect mine," she said, giving him a long look.

"I think I'll take the sculpture, it's beautiful," he said, turning his attention back to the crystal figurine on the table, "can you wrap it for me?"

Picking up the figurine, she headed towards the counter. "Yes, if you'll just step to the counter, you can pay for it and I will wrap it for you."

Following her to the counter, he paid cash for the figure. She placed the figure in a padded box, and then wrapped it in gossamer tissue paper. As she handed him the box, their fingers briefly touched, sending an electric-like current through the both of them.

Sophie's eyes widened for a moment, she looked at Nick's face, trying to see if he had noticed, but his face gave nothing away. She turned quickly back to the cash receipt book, wrote out the receipt and handed it to him, careful not to let their fingers touch again.

"Thank you for coming into the shop today. Good luck with the gift, I know she'll love it," she said, smiling.

"I know she will, how could she not?" Nick smiled mysteriously at her and headed for the door.

She watched him leave the shop, a look of puzzlement on her face. Shrugging, she put away the receipt book and headed over to the window. She was just in time to see a large black 4x4 truck pull away from the curb. She smiled to herself in satisfaction, *just as she thought, a macho truck for a macho man.* Shaking her head, she headed towards the front of the shop, mentally going over her appointments for the afternoon.

"Well, well, isn't that interesting, you know, he is rather handsome in an arrogant sort of way," a voice said from the direction of the alcove.

"Well, in my opinion, just because he's good looking, doesn't mean he's a nice guy," a second voice chimed in.

"All right, you two, what's going on? I've never known either one of you to be that quiet for so long," Sophie said, crossing her arms in front of her. "Just what are you two up to now?"

Ann floated across the floor to stand in front of Sophie. "Well, he is absolutely gorgeous, there's no denying that. However, he does need a little bit of an attitude adjustment, I'll grant you that. Now if it were me, I'd have asked him out for lunch or something."

"Ann, remember what I said earlier, and mind your manners," Martha said, looking at her meaningfully.

"Okay, okay, I get it, but you must admit, he does have a nice butt," she said, rolling her eyes. "Jeez, I can't have any fun around here."

"OK, you two, give; what's up with the silent treatment? Something must be up, because you're never that quiet."

"What makes you think something's up just because we're quiet?" Ann asked, trying to look innocent.

Raising her eyebrow at Ann, Sophie continued as if she hadn't spoken. "So when are you going to tell me what's going on? Don't try to tell me it's nothing, because I won't believe you," she said, crossing her arms over chest.

"Well, we didn't want to get in the way of your making a big sale. I know how important that sale is to you, and how much it will help Brittany. We know she's saving to get her guide dog," Martha said.

"You're right, of course; that reminds me, I had better call her and let her know about the sale," Sophie said. Heading for the phone behind the counter, she quickly dialed Brittany's number. The phone rang several times, then Brittany answered, "Hello?"

"Hey Bree, it's Sophie. You know that really big angel figurine we've been trying to sell?"

"Oh, do you mean the one with the moon and stars attached?"

"Yeah, that's the one. Well, guess what? I sold it!"

A squeal of delight emanated from the other end of the phone. "So how much did you get for it? I know $400 is a big chunk of money, but I did put a lot of work into it."

"I didn't sell it for $400."

"Oh, well even $300 or $350 would be great right now."

"Well, I guess you'll just have to settle for $600," Sophie said.

"What? You're kidding, right? How much did you really get for it?"

"No, I'm not kidding. I actually got $600 for it."

"Oh my gosh, that's so wonderful. That will give me the rest of the money for my service dog, with some left over. Thank you so much, Sophie, this means the world to me."

"I know, it's wonderful, and the figurine was worth every bit of that $600. I'll drop the money by on my way to the store tonight so you can have it for tomorrow. You better call the guide dog facility and let them know that you'll be picking up your dog ASAP."

"You're right, I better get off here and give them a call. I'm so excited, I can hardly stand it. I'll give you a call as soon as I find out when I'm getting my dog."

"All right, let me know when you're ready to pick up your dog, and I'll take you. Do you know if it's a boy or girl?"

"It's a boy, and his name is Zeus. He's an unusual breed for a guide dog. He's a pit bull, he's gentle with the heart of a warrior."

"He sounds just perfect for you. As we both know pit bulls get a bum rap, but we're working to change that! I can hardly wait to meet him," Sophie said and hung up the phone.

Chapter 3

Climbing into the cab of his truck, Nick used the seat belt to strap the box holding the crystalline sculpture into the passenger seat. Pausing for a moment, he frowned as a pair of mysterious golden eyes filled his mind. Shaking off the vision, he started the truck and headed for his office. It suddenly occurred to him that he hadn't accomplished what he had set out to do. He failed to confront the woman in the shop about bilking old ladies out of their money. He had been completely sidetracked, what was wrong with him? It was so unlike him to be distracted from something once he had made up his mind to do whatever it was. He was angry at himself for being so easily sidetracked and angry at the woman with the topaz eyes for making him forget what he had set out to do.

She wasn't even his type, for God's sake, he sighed disgustedly, running his hand through his hair. He'd have to figure out a way to expose her for the money grubbing person that she is.

By the time he got to his office, he was in a terrible mood. One look at his face told his secretary it was not going to be a good day. Glaring at her as he walked in, he barked out an order. "Get Jason on the line, Adele, I need an update on the Baxter building, now." He slammed his office door shut with a loud thud.

"Well, what's got his shorts in a knot? That meeting he had this morning must not have gone well," she muttered to herself as she dialed Jason's number. After what seemed like an eternity, Jason answered.

"Jason, it's Adele. How's it going on the Baxter project?"

"Fine, why? What's up?" he wanted to know.

"Nick just got here, and he's behaving like a bear with a sore head. I just wanted to warn you before you spoke to him."

"Well, everything here is fine; in fact, we're a little ahead of schedule. The building is gutted, and the internal framing is complete. The electricians and plumbers are starting today. It's unusual that everything has come together without a hitch like this." He chuckled. "It's almost as if the stars are in alignment or something. Better put him on, might as well get it over with. Thanks for the warning, you're a sweetheart."

"Tell me that after he gets through with you!" she muttered to him.

Pushing the intercom button, she informed Nick Jason was on the line. She sure wished she knew what had happened at his morning meeting. Hell, she didn't even know if the meeting this morning was business or personal. All he would say was to mark him out until lunch, that he had a very important meeting this morning. She had asked him if he needed a file, but he told her he didn't, which didn't really tell her anything. She sighed and got back to work.

Picking up the phone, Nick punched the blinking line and barked into the receiver, "Jason, what's happening with the project? It had better be on time."

There was silence on the other end of the line for a moment or two. Nick sighed upon hearing the silence. "Sorry, Jason, it's been one of those mornings. I didn't mean to take it out on you. Are we on track for completion by the end of the month?"

"That's okay, Nick, I understand completely. Brenda and I were up a good portion of the night with the baby; he's teething, and he doesn't sleep well because of it. Well, I've got some good news for you, it looks like we're actually ahead of schedule. It's a funny thing, Nick, a couple of days ago we couldn't get either the plumbers or electricians to come in until mid-month. Then I get a call this morning from both of them, saying that they'll be in this afternoon. It's really bizarre, like suddenly all the planets fell into alignment or something." He laughed.

Nick winced at Jason's comment about the planets, thinking of his meeting this morning. "Well, that's great news, because I just got the news that we won that bid for that new condominium complex. That's a really big job, and it will keep us busy for the next year. I'll have to get busy and hire at least another thirty people for the job. This will definitely help out the economy and put some people back to work."

"That's great, Nick, there's nothing like job security. Who you gonna get to take on the foreman job? Whoever you get had better have a lot of experience, patience and the hide like a rhino." He laughed.

"Well, I was thinking about offering you the position of project foreman."

There was a moment of silence on the other end of the line.

"You still with me, Jason?" Nick asked.

"Yeah, I'm still here; you just took me by surprise, that's all. Do you mean it, Nick? You want me to be in charge of such a big project? It's not that I can't do it, of course, I just want you to be sure that you have the right man for the job."

Sounding suddenly serious, Nick said, "I mean it, 'J', there's no one else that I would trust with such a big project. Will you do it? Maybe you shouldn't answer right now; take a few days to think about it and talk it over with Brenda."

"Thanks, Nick, I do want this job, but you're right, I definitely need to talk to Brenda about it. I'll let you know Friday for sure. When are we due to start?"

"We're gonna start the end of this month, so we've got a lot to do and a short time to do it in. If you're gonna take on the job, I'll want you to be in on the hiring, but I'll have the final say. By the way, a substantial raise goes with your new position."

"Sounds good to me, and it's about time the economy started to pick up. New building is definitely a sign that the economy is on the upswing."

"I agree, it's about time, and we're going to reap the rewards. We've been lucky enough to have work and not lose anyone these last three years. It hasn't been easy, but doing these renovation projects has really saved our butts. You have to change with the times, or you go under. Okay, 'J', I gotta get back to work. I'll talk to you on Friday."

Hanging up the phone, Nick's mind wandered back over the past three years. It had been rough, what with the economy and trying to keep the business afloat. He was luckier than most, because his company was well-established. They were well known in the Pacific Northwest and had a good reputation, so he managed to snag a lot of smaller jobs to subsidize the lack of bigger projects. Then there was his father's heart attack a couple of years ago and his death six months ago. His mother's grief and depression had him worried; it was as if she had withdrawn from life.

Over the last couple of months, he had noticed a distinct change in her demeanor. She seemed more like her old self, full of life and even spending time away from the house with her friends. Ultimately, he would have to confront his mother about the fortune teller. He was not looking forward to doing it.

The intercom rang, bringing his thoughts back to the present. "Yes, what is it Adele?"

"Pamela's on line two. Do you want me to take a message, or will you take it?"

"No, I'll get it, thanks." Sighing, he picked up the phone.

"Pamela, what a surprise, I didn't expect to hear from you until Friday. To what do I owe the pleasure of this phone call?"

"Well, darling, I just received an invitation to that new Broadway play that's going to be starting Saturday night. A certain percentage of the proceeds are going to a local animal charity, and I know how you love to support local charities," she said.

"And what show is that? I'm afraid you have to refresh my memory; it's been pretty hectic around here." He had absolutely no idea what play she was talking about.

"It's an updated version of West Side Story, and it's supposed to be absolutely wonderful. I know you don't really care for musicals, but since this is a classic, I thought you might like to see it."

"I'll have to check and make sure there's nothing on my calendar for Saturday night. I'll give you a call back tomorrow and let you know for sure if I can make it."

"Oh, all right, I'll wait to hear from you then," she replied, sounding petulant.

She definitely sounded put out by the fact that he didn't readily agree to go to the play. For the first time in their relationship, he was questioning where she thought their relationship was heading. He told her from the beginning that he wasn't up for a long-term relationship. He made it clear that he wanted someone who looked good on his arm, was physically compatible, but who did not want any strings attached. Maybe this was as good a time as any to start easing out of the relationship. It just occurred to him that their relationship had run its course and she had just given him a perfect out. The phone on his desk rang, breaking him out of his thoughts.

The day passed in a flurry of activity, and before he knew it Adele was popping her head in the door to let him know that she was leaving.

"Nick, your mom called and she asked me to remind you you're supposed to come for dinner tonight and you had better not be late. I'm heading out. I'll see you in the morning."

It had completely slipped his mind that he was going to his mother's for dinner tonight. He knew there would be hell to pay if he was late. Looking at his watch, he realized if he didn't want to be late, he would have to leave right away. Sighing, he turned his computer off, gathered his things, and headed for the door.

Chapter 4

Just as Sophie hung up the phone, she heard the bell over the door go off and knew that her next appointment had just arrived. "Don't think you're off the hook, we'll talk about this later," she said telepathically to Martha and Ann.

Heading for the door, she greeted her client and led her over to the little alcove where she did her readings.

"Wow, that was close, saved by the bell. It's a good thing she's got readings scheduled all day," Ann said to Martha.

"Don't think we're out of the woods yet; she's not one to forget about what happened, so we had better come up with a plausible reason for our silence," Martha warned.

Ann was soon distracted by the guides who accompanied the woman for her reading. Shaking her head, Martha searched her mind for a plausible excuse as to why they weren't hanging around as usual. Then she remembered that every now and then she had to report to Michael, the archangel, on the progress of her trainees. Sophie already knew that this had to be done on a regular basis. So it was the perfect excuse for their absence.

She signaled for Ann to return to her so she could let her know what she was going to tell Sophie. Excusing herself from the other guides, she returned to Martha's side.

"Is something wrong, Martha?"

"No, I just thought of what we're going to tell Sophie as to why we were gone."

"That's great, what are you going to tell her?"

"She knows that I need to give Michael progress reports on how you're doing."

"Don't remind me," Ann interjected.

"I'm going to tell her that we were summoned by Michael to give our progress report. That should stop her from asking more questions."

"How come we can't let her know that we saw Nick and the others?"

"Let's go outside; we can't talk here." Walking through the wall, Martha led the way to the old porch swing located on the back lawn of the shop. Taking a seat on the swing, Martha began to explain to Ann the reason for the secrecy.

"As you know, guides and guardians are privy to the intimate details of a person's life, including their future."

"Sure, I know that," Ann said, and then a thought occurred to her. "You're not saying that Sophie and Nick have a future together, are you?" she asked incredulously.

Sighing, she responded, "Yes, that is exactly what I'm saying. I don't want to be accused of interfering in her life. Things need to unfold as they're meant to with, no interference from us. It's very important for you to understand when you need to nudge things along, and when you need to just step back. When you're assigned to someone, you know their future events."

"Oh, I see what you're saying; if you told her, for example, that Joe Blow was going to be her husband, then it could alter the events."

"Yes, that's right, and you would be interfering with their free will, and that we are not allowed to do. We also have intimate knowledge of all our charges' future major life events."

"Are Sophie and Nick going to meet again? I've got a feeling we haven't seen the last of him," Ann commented.

"Yes, they are definitely going to meet again," Martha said with a secretive smile.

"I know that smile; you've got something up your sleeve, and you're not about to let me in on it."

"Looks like Sophie's done with the reading," Martha noted.

After seeing her client to the door, she felt the presence of her guides close by. "All right, you two, so where were you this morning?"

"I was summoned by Michael to give him a report on Ann's progress. It's been a while since we last checked in," Martha told her.

"Oh sorry, I guess it has been a while since he last summoned you. I'm just so used to you being with me that I sometimes forget you have other duties as well as watching over me. I hope he's pleased with Ann's progress."

"Yes, he's quite pleased with how she's doing."

"Good, I'm glad. You missed all the excitement this morning. I think the man who bought the figurine had an ulterior motive, but I can't figure out what it is. Oh well, time will tell."

"When will you be taking Bree to pick up her dog?" Martha asked.

"Hopefully, he'll be ready this weekend. If he is, then we'll pick him up Saturday afternoon. Knowing Bree, I'm sure she'll want to be there first thing in the morning to pick him up."

"So who bought the figurine? It has to be someone with money, and those are far and few between around here," Ann asked. Martha gave her a warning look.

"It's kind of weird, this guy came into the shop, said he was looking for a birthday present. I don't think that was his original intention, though; something just didn't ring true with him. I can't quite put my finger on it, but it's almost as if he had a hidden agenda," she mused, more to herself than them.

"Maybe he's seen you somewhere else and wanted to meet you. Is he good looking? Oh, I can see by the image in your mind that he was definitely good looking," Ann said with a smile.

"Yes, he was definitely good looking, but he's a non-believer. I doubt if I'll ever see him again anyway," she said with a smile. She stood lost in thought for a few moments, remembering the tall man with the coal black hair. The ringing of the phone brought her thoughts back to the present.

Reaching for the phone, she was pleasantly surprised to hear Jewel's voice.

"Hello, Sophie, this is Jewel."

"Hello, Jewel, good to hear from you. Did you ever find the box you were looking for?"

"Did you ever find the box you were looking for?"

"Oh yes, I certainly did, and I wanted to thank you so much for all your help."

"Don't thank me; your husband told me where to find it, and I just relayed his message."

"Well, without you I never would have found it by myself," she said earnestly.

"It's all part of the work that I do, and I'm glad I could help out."

"I'm calling to invite you to dinner next weekend, will you come?"

"I would love to have dinner with you, but I need to bring JT with me, if that's okay? He hates to be left alone in the evenings."

"Of course, dear, bring him along. I love that dog of yours, he has such a gentle soul. How about six-thirty next Sunday, will that work for you? I live in Laurelhurst, I'll text you the address."

"Yes, that will give me enough time to get there with all the weekend traffic."

"Great, we'll see you then," she said, hanging up.

She said we, I wonder if she's inviting someone else, she wondered but shrugged it off and got back to work cleaning the shop.

The day passed in a whirlwind of clients and cleaning. As the last client left, Sophie let out a sigh of relief. Looking at her watch, she realized it was a little after 4pm and she was late closing the shop. Locking the shop door, she turned out the lights as she headed towards the back of the shop, with JT following closely on her heels. Opening the ornate door at the back of the shop, she climbed the stairs to her apartment on the second floor. Turning on the lights, she made her way into the bedroom and changed her clothes. Heading to the kitchen, she pulled out some ground chicken and browned it in the pan, adding spices and rice to create a light dinner for herself and JT.

"JT, get your dish for Mama."

The dog immediately went over to the far end of the kitchen and picked up the red bowl marked 'JT', bringing it over to her.

"Thank you, you're such a good boy," she said, taking the bowl from him and rubbing his ears. Filling the bowl with most of the cooked mixture, she sat it down on the floor for him. Taking a couple of tortilla shells, shredded lettuce and cheese from the refrigerator, she made a wrap, grabbed a glass of milk and sat down at the kitchen table to eat her dinner.

"How's your dinner, JT?" The dog looked up, licking his chops. Grinning at him, she finished her dinner and cleaned up the kitchen.

Heading for the living room, she grabbed her computer and sat down on the couch to reconcile the books and read her emails. The couch sagged as JT climbed up next to her and made himself comfortable. Reaching over, she rubbed his ears absentmindedly. After a while, JT became restless.

"Mom, I really need to go outside, can you let me outside now?" JT asked telepathically.

"I'm sorry, big man, of course you can," she told him telepathically. Setting aside the computer, she looked at the clock. "Oh my garsh, its 9 o'clock already, I get so involved in what I'm doing that I forget about the time. It's a good thing I have you to keep me grounded."

Going down the back stairs, she let JT out and waited for his return. Just as he was coming back in, the phone rang. Looking at the Caller ID, she saw it was Brittany calling.

"Hello, Bree, how are you?"

"I wanted to let you know we can pick up Zeus Saturday, if that's all right with you?"

"Sure, no problem, let me check my schedule here," she said, looking at her schedule on her computer. "It looks like I'm free after 12 o'clock, if that's okay with you?"

"Yes, they said I could come and get him anytime I wanted tomorrow, so I'll give them a call in the morning and let them know when we're coming."

"All right, I'll leave here at 12:15 and should get to your place by 12:20. See you Saturday." Heading for the bathroom, she completed her nightly routine of removing her makeup and brushing her teeth. She climbed into her big king-sized bed. JT wandered around to the other side of the bed and took up his favorite spot at the foot of the bed.

"Goodnight, big man."

JT let out a huge sigh and almost immediately started snoring. Smiling to herself, she snuggled deeper into the sheets and fell fast asleep.

Chapter 5

Getting into his truck, he paused as a pair of golden eyes floated into his mind. Shaking off the thought, he put the truck in gear and headed for his mother's house. Arriving at her house, he noticed that his brother was already home. This in itself was unusual for him; on Monday, he usually played cards at his club. Either this was a special occasion, or he was sick, and since no one had a birthday this month, he was not sure what was going on.

Entering the house, he could hear voices coming from the back of the house and the smell of his favorite food, dolmadas, filled the air. Entering the kitchen, he noticed the smile on his mother's face as Matt teased her about something.

"Hey, big brother, it's about time you got here. I'm getting hungry, and Mom said we couldn't eat until you got here. Here I am dying of starvation, and she won't let me eat," Matt said, placing his hand over his stomach for dramatic effect.

"You'll survive, little brother," he said, grinning.

"All right, boys, you have to earn your supper, so go set the table," she said, waving them out of the kitchen.

"All right, all right, we're going, don't get your panties in a twist!" Matt said, laughing, as he left the kitchen behind his brother.

Entering the dining room, they got out the everyday china and started setting the table.

"Hey, what's the special occasion?" Nick asked.

Shrugging, Matt started laying out the place settings. "She asked me to skip the club tonight because you were coming over for dinner. When I asked her what was up, she just clammed up and told me I would find out the same time you did."

"I wonder what this is all about? Oh, well," he said, shrugging, "it gave me the perfect excuse to tell Pamela I couldn't come over for drinks. She was having a few friends over tonight, and you know what that means."

"Yeah, the place will be packed with snooty people all trying to impress each other with their wealth. Sounds like she's becoming a little too demanding to me, and that means you're going to dump her. She won't be happy about it, and she won't melt quietly into the background. I'll bet she tells everyone that she dumped you so she can save face."

"I don't really care. She knew my terms when we got together, I made it quite clear. It will only be her pride that gets hurt, nothing more."

Matt grinned. "Oh, how I'd love to be a fly on the wall when she finds out."

Nick smiled mischievously at his brother. "Do you want me to record it for you?"

"Would you?" he asked excitedly.

Nick rolled his eyes at him. "No, I was just kidding."

Matt looked so disappointed, Nick had to laugh. "Besides, you really don't want to hear those kind of words coming out of someone like her. It would probably give you nightmares."

They both laughed as their mom came into the room carrying the main dinner course.

"What's so funny, boys? I hope it was a clean joke," she said, smiling. She sat the platter in the center of the table. "All right, boys, there's more dishes to bring in, so everyone grab one and bring it in. Oh, and Nick, can you get a bottle of your dad's favorite wine out of the cellar for dinner?"

He was surprised at his mother's request but managed to hold his tongue. Heading down to the cool cellar, he picked out one of his father's favorite local wines. He loved to support local vendors, and Willamette Valley wines were a favorite of his. As he climbed the stairs, he stopped halfway up. He could have sworn he heard his father's voice. Shaking off the thought, he continued upstairs.

Arriving back in the dining room, he noticed an envelope sitting next to his mother's place setting. "You can do the honors of opening the wine, Matthew," she said, handing him the corkscrew opener.

Opening the wine, he poured everyone a glass and sat down. "I'll say grace, Mom," he offered.

"Thank you, Matthew."

Finishing grace, everyone started eating. Halfway through dinner, Nick asked, "So what's the special occasion, Mom?"

"Yeah, what's this all about? Are we celebrating something?"

"Yes, we are celebrating something, something that's been a long time coming," she said, smiling.

"Well, don't keep us in suspense, let us in on the secret," Matt said, smiling at her.

"All right, but first I need to give you a little background. When your father and I got married, things were pretty tight financially for us. Just after you were born, Nick, your father decided to start his own construction company. Little by little, our finances got better. One day, your father came to me with what I considered to be a harebrained idea."

"I've never known Dad to do anything questionable, he's always been a guy with an eye to make the most of things in business," Nick said, defending his father.

"Nick, you only see what he had become by the time you were old enough to understand about the business. There was a side to him that he rarely showed, that of a dreamer. I know you don't believe me, but when he was young, he fell for a couple of moneymaking schemes." She smiled as she saw the look on her sons' faces.

"Okay, so Dad made a couple of bad deals. In the end, he came out okay," Nick insisted.

"After the first couple of bad deals, your father and I agreed that if he was going to invest in anything off the wall, we would talk about it first. But one day while I was out grocery shopping, Sam, an old friend of his, came over. He told your father that a couple of young men were starting up a computer company that he was sure would be a big success. He felt these guys had a great idea, computer software that anyone could learn to use, he felt it couldn't fail. He must have talked a good talk, because before I got back from the store, your father had given him thirty thousand dollars to invest in the company. When he finally told me about it a couple of months later, I was absolutely livid."

"I just can't believe that Dad would do something like that, no wonder you were mad!" Matt said.

"It took me a while to get over what he did. Over the years, he tried to talk to me about it, but I just wouldn't listen. A couple of months before he died, he wrote me a letter to be opened after his death."

"I didn't know that, what did it say?" Nick wanted to know.

Opening the large manila envelope beside her plate, she produced a smaller white envelope. "Here, you can read it for yourself," she said, handing it to Nick.

"Read it out loud so I know what it says, too," Matt told him.

Opening the envelope, he took out the single piece of lined paper and read it.

"My darling, if you're reading this, I am gone. Remember all those years ago when you were so mad at me for making that large investment with Sam? I'm sure you do, as you didn't speak to me for a whole week. Well, a few years ago I did a little follow up on the investment that I made that day, and it turns out Sam was right about it. The names of the two fellows who started the company might ring a bell with you now, Paul Welch and Richard Blane. Their company is known as Computek. You see, my dear, I did make a good investment after all. At my last contact with our investor, my investment is now worth over 1 million dollars. I have placed the papers with the proof of investment in a secure lock box in our room. I love you, Bill."

"Wow, Mom, where are the papers? We have to take a look at them," Matt said excitedly.

"Well, that's just it. I had been trying to find the lock box since your father died. The key was in the envelope, but I couldn't find the box. I tore apart our whole bedroom looking for it, with no success."

Deep in thought, Nick suddenly spoke up, "Did Dad give you any idea where he might have put the box?"

"No, I spent the first four months after your father's death turning the whole house upside down, with no success. Then Jane and I went to lunch one afternoon, and she told me about a woman she goes to, a psychic named Sophie."

"You don't believe in those people, do you? They're only after your money, Mom, don't tell me you've been giving this woman money?" he said angrily. The look on his mother's face stopped anything further that he was going to say. She looked supremely confident and unaffected by his outburst. This was another side of his mother that he had never seen before.

"Nicholas Stavros, you are interrupting me, so just sit down and shut up!"

Nick was so surprised by his mother's commanding voice, he did just that. He could hear his brother snickering under his breath and glared at him. Instead of having the desired effect of shutting him up, it made him laugh even harder.

"Matthew, please be quiet so I can finish telling you about Sophie," his mother said sternly. He managed to stop laughing long enough for his mother to continue her story.

"Now as I was saying, Jane suggested that I come with her to see Sophie for a reading. She is a medium, which means she can speak with those who have crossed over. I went with Jane, and the moment I sat down for the reading, your father came through. She told me that he had a message for me." Glancing at Nick, she held up her hand to silence him before he could open his mouth. "Contrary to popular belief, I am not so naive as to believe everything I hear. I sat down and didn't say a word, I decided that I wouldn't tell her anything but the basics. The moment I sat down, she told me that Bill was coming through. She asked me if I had found the lock box yet. Well, you could have knocked me over with a feather. I told her that I had not been able to find it yet. She then proceeds to tell me to look in our bedroom behind the ornate mirror.

"When I told her that I had already looked there, she told me that Bill said to press on the wall behind the mirror right in the center of the paneling, and a door would pop open. She said I would need to press real hard. So I came home and did just that. At first it didn't open, but when I put my whole weight on it, it sprung open and there inside the wall was the box. I got the key out of my jewelry box and opened it up.

"Inside was an envelope with the papers he spoke about in the letter. I didn't say anything to either of you earlier because I wanted to have them authenticated first." Handing the envelope with the papers in it to Nick, she smiled serenely and said, "I took the papers to our lawyers, and they researched them and assured me they are absolutely authentic."

"Holy mother of God, Mom, they're worth a fortune!" Matthew said excitedly.

"What do you plan on doing with the stocks, Mom?" Nick asked quietly.

"I'm going to cash them in and reinvest half of the money into the business, and I want to put some into a trust account for my future grandchildren. I'll keep a small amount for myself and give both of you a share."

"Mom, neither one of us is married, let alone looking for a wife. You might as well use some of it to take a trip or something," Matt told her.

"I think Matt has a good idea, Mom, take a trip; you've always wanted to see where Dad grew up in Greece," Nick reminded her.

"I had always planned to visit his home with him by my side. Now that he's gone, I have no interest in going," she said sadly.

Nick and Matt remained silent, both remembering how their father wanted to take her to see where he grew up. Now he would never take her.

"So you say a medium told you where to find the papers? I find it hard to believe that a stranger would have that kind of information," Nick said, looking his mother in the eye.

"Nicholas Stavros, are you accusing me of lying?" she asked, outrage clearly written all over her face.

The look in his mother's eyes told him she wasn't lying and that her Irish temper had reached the boiling point. He remembered being on the receiving end of her temper a few times as a teenager, and it was not very pleasant. "All right, Mom, I'm sorry. So who is this medium? I never knew you believed in all that mumbo jumbo."

"Nickolas, I'm Irish, and we believe in the little people. Now why wouldn't I believe in mediums? Your grandmother and great-grandmother were what we call fey. I myself have some of these abilities; not as strong as they did, mind you, but they're there nonetheless."

"Mom, are you going to sell all the stock or keep some? I think you should keep some, because it will only go up," Matt advised her.

"I agree, you can sell some and retain a small amount of the stock. When were you thinking about selling the stock?" Nick asked.

"I already have someone looking into the selling of it. You know Gavin, don't you, Nick?"

"Yes, you chose a good man, Mom. He'll get you the best price for those stocks. Let me know how it goes," he said, handing the envelope back to her.

The talk became general after that, and the evening passed quietly. Saying his goodnight to his mother, he got in his truck and headed home to his house.

Pulling into the driveway of his home, he activated the garage door remote and pulled his truck in next to his Chrysler 300. Climbing out of the truck, he heard a deep woof from the other side of the door leading to the inside of the house. Smiling, he closed the garage door and headed for the security keypad next to the inside door. Punching in the alarm code, he opened the door to find his Doberman, Max, waiting impatiently for him.

"Hey there, boy, how was your day?" he asked, rubbing his ears. "I know I'm late, but I'll make it up to you. I'm sure Juanita gave you your big steak for your dinner, but I brought you a little something from Mom's house." The dog's eyes seemed to light up, and if possible, he wiggled his stub even harder.

He placed the sack that his mother sent home with him on the kitchen counter. Max's nose picked up on the scent, and he sat down in front of the bag. Smiling at the dog, Nick said, "Give me a minute to get changed, and I'll give you your treat."

Heading for the bedroom, he changed into his workout clothes and returned to the kitchen. As he walked into the kitchen, he could see that Max had not moved from the spot where he sat down. Grinning, Nick opened the bag and pulled out a large ham shank wrapped in plastic wrap. Unwrapping the plastic wrap, he handed the bone to the waiting dog. Max very carefully took the bone from Nick's hand and headed over to the far corner of the kitchen. Nick had created an area in the corner of the kitchen with a washable pad where Max knew to go to eat.

Heading down to the basement, Nick turned on the stereo and climbed onto the treadmill. An hour later, he finished his workout and noticed that Max had settled himself on his overstuffed bed by the stairs. The funny thing was, Max was looking at the large futon couch with his ears up and his head cocked to one side. It looked as if he was listening to something or someone that only he could see. Then his stub of a tail started to wiggle madly and he let out a low woof.

"What's wrong with me?" he thought to himself, "there's no one here but him and I." Suddenly, a thought occurred to him. "Dad, is that you? Are you there? If you're there, can you do something to let me know?" He waited for a moment, and when nothing happened he shook his head. "I must be as crazy as that woman."

Suddenly, there was a bang from the direction of the fireplace. Turning, he noticed a picture had fallen forward onto the mantel. *That's odd*, he thought, *there wasn't supposed to be any pictures on the mantel, only a couple of bookends*. Walking over to the picture, he picked it up and noticed that it was a picture of his father and himself his mother had taken a year before his death. But the picture didn't belong down there, it was always kept on his desk upstairs. Taking the picture back upstairs, he returned it to where it belonged.

Juanita, his housekeeper, must have left it downstairs when she was cleaning. Suddenly, he thought he heard a voice say, "Are you sure?" Startled, he looked around the room. Finding no one there, he shook his head to clear it. The more he thought about the picture, the more he became obsessed with finding out how it got there.

Sitting down at his desk, he pushed the speed dial number on the speaker phone for his housekeeper. The number rang a couple of times, and Juanita answered.

"Hello, Nick, is something wrong?"

"No, Juanita, nothing's wrong. I just have a quick question to ask. You know that picture I have on my desk of my father and I?"

"Sure, I know the one. I just dusted it this morning."

"This is going to sound strange, but I was wondering if you might have carried the picture downstairs by accident today?"

"No, Nick, I always start cleaning in the downstairs and work my way up. I dusted it this morning and sat it back down on your desk. So you found it downstairs? Hmm, do you ever use your dad's coffee cup?"

"No, I don't want to break it by accident, so I don't use it, why?"

"I know this is going to sound strange, but ever since he passed, I find his cup sitting next to the coffee pot. It happens like clockwork every morning when I come in to clean. I always put it back in the cupboard again. If you want my opinion, I think he just wants us to know he's still here."

There was silence on the other end of the line, and for a moment she thought she might have said too much.

"You know something, Juanita, I'm beginning to think you may be on to something," he said gruffly.

"Have you ever seen his coffee cup sitting out since he died?"

"No. Until you told me, I hadn't a clue, but then I probably would have brushed it off anyway." He laughed.

"Why don't you ask him to put his cup on the counter for you tonight and see what happens? It couldn't hurt, maybe you'll be surprised."

"It sure would be nice if I knew he could hear me on some level." He sighed.

"I know you miss him. My grandmother used to tell me to be careful what I wished for. Goodnight, Nick."

"Goodnight, Juanita." Hanging up the phone, he realized that their conversation had raised more questions than it answered. Max whined and nudged his arm. Reaching down, he rubbed his ears. Heading back into the kitchen to get a glass of water, he noticed the answering machine blinking. Pushing the button, he listened to the messages. The first one was a hang up, but the second one was from Pamela.

"I just wanted to remind you about the opera on Friday night. Don't forget to pick me up around six. We can have dinner and then head over to the concert hall."

"Damn, I forgot all about that. I wish there was a way to get out of it," he said, sighing.

The dog whined, and Nick turned to him and smiled. "Well, boy, I think it's time for bed. We have to get up early tomorrow morning and get a run in. How would you like to go with me to work tomorrow? I'll be out in the field, and I know how you love to ride in the truck."

Whining and wiggling his stub, the dog woofed softly in agreement.

Finishing his water, he turned off the lights and headed for the bedroom. After taking a shower, he slid into bed and heaved a sigh of relief. The last thing he saw before he fell asleep was a pair of laughing topaz eyes.

"Well, do you think I got through to him?" Nick's father, Bill, wanted to know.

Bert looked at the man standing opposite him with the thin build, brown eyes, stark white hair and asked, "Bill, you know your son better than anyone. Do you really think it's going to be that easy to convince him that you're still hanging around?"

He thought for a moment, then grinned. "You're right about that; he's just as stubborn as I am."

"I've got an idea, Bill," Helen chimed in, "why don't you go into his dreams and talk to him?"

"That will never work, luv, he'll just think it's his imagination and blow it off. Why don't you put your coffee cup on the nightstand by the bed? When he wakes up and sees your cup right there, he'll have his proof."

"That's a great idea, Sid. He'll have physical proof that I'm trying to communicate with him. What do you think, Bert?"

"As you say, it's a great idea."

"What are we going to do about that Pamela woman?" Helen wanted to know.

"Not to worry, luv, she's on her way out. By the sound of it, she's getting a little too possessive for his liking," Sid told her.

"I don't like her, she's worse than all of his other women. This one's got her eye on his money, and once she finds out about the Computek shares, it will be even worse."

"Cool your jets, luv, how's she going to find out about them?"

"In case you don't remember, her friend Toni works for the family lawyer. If she doesn't know already, she will shortly," Helen said with a frown.

"Sorry, luv, I forgot all about that," Sid said, shrugging.

Rolling her eyes, Helen turned to Bert. "Well, what are we going to do about this little state of affairs?"

"Nothing," Bert replied quietly.

"Nothing, are you crazy?" she fairly screeched at Bert.

Bert raised an eyebrow and looked meaningfully at her. The look was enough to silence anything else she was about to say.

Looking repentant, she mumbled, "Sorry, I didn't mean to yell."

"You need to learn when to step back and let things play out," he told her. "If you give some mortals enough rope, they will hang themselves with it, and this woman is one of those. She thinks that she is in control of her life and Nick's. She'll find out soon enough that control is only an illusion," he said, smiling serenely.

She wasn't sure what Bert was up to, but she definitely liked the twinkle she saw in his eye. So she had to be content to watch and see how the situation unfolded. Sid, on the other hand, was enjoying watching her squirm.

"I definitely cannot stand the woman; she's too condescending, and I think Sophie would be a better choice for him," Bill informed them.

"Don't worry, Bill, everything will work itself out, you'll see," Bert assured him.

"I guess I'll just have to sit back and watch what happens. Although by the sound of it, Pamela has run her course with Nick."

"I agree, old man. I think he has her number, but I've seen plenty birds cause big problems on the way out. I think Helen's right, we need to keep our defenses up. Can't help but feel sorry for the guides who have to watch after that one."

"All right, Sid, it's time for us to check in with Gabe and let him know how your training is going.

Helen, Bill, keep a low profile and stay out of trouble while we're gone."

"Don't worry, Bert, there's not much happening on this end anyway. I think I'll go see my wife while you're gone."

"That's fine, Bill, she could probably use a visit from you. I'll see you when I get back," he said, disappearing.

"I'll be back in a little while, Helen."

Helen watched as he walked off, heading for his wife's house. Sighing, she headed for the couch and tried to focus in on Pamela's guides. She connected enough to know that she had two female guides. Suddenly, it was like a door shut in her face and the connection was broken. She figured it was Bert keeping her from doing something he thought was stupid. So, she settled down and tuned in on her sister for a long gab session.

Chapter 6

Sophie woke to a cold, wet nose moving over her cheek. Without opening her eyes, she mumbled, "Morning, do you want to go outside?" she asked the persistent wet-nosed dog.

A soft "woof" was her only verbal answer.

Opening her eyes, she looked at the clock and saw JT had woken her up at his usual time of 5:30 am. "I don't suppose just once you'd let me sleep in," she asked him, knowing it was a rhetorical question. "All right, let me get my robe and put my slippers on."

She grabbed her robe off the bedpost and looked around for her slippers. Catching sight of one on the other side of the bedroom, she looked around for the second one, finding it on the end of the bed next to where JT had been sleeping. Picking up the slipper off the bed, she noticed it was extremely damp. The slipper was covered in drool. Putting her hands on her hips, she frowned at the dog.

"I thought we had an agreement that you weren't going to chew on my slippers?" she reminded him.

"Yes, we did, and as you will see, I didn't chew on them; only carried them around and slept with them," he told her telepathically.

Checking the slippers, she noticed they were damp where he had carried them in his mouth but otherwise intact. "All right, I'll give you that, but please do try not to drool on them too much. It's not fun to stick my feet into soggy slippers." Placing the slippers on the floor, she pushed her feet into them.

They felt cold and soggy, a very unpleasant sensation. Pulling them off, she decided she would rather go barefoot. Letting JT outside, she headed to the bathroom to take a quick shower.

By the time she had gotten out of the shower, she could hear JT knocking at the door. She had learned that if you leave the screen door latch up, he would use his paw and bounce it against the frame, causing a knocking sound. This was his not so subtle way of telling you he was ready to come in. Heading down the backstairs, she let him in.

"How about some breakfast?" she asked him. Letting out a mooing sound, he agreed to her suggestion. Putting some of his favorite soft foods into his bowl, she made some coffee for herself.

"We have a couple of cats coming in today that need me to speak to their owners. You need to stay outside while they're here, for some reason you make them nervous." She smiled at him and rubbed his ears. "Let's go to the store before our appointments begin at 10 o'clock."

Heading into the bedroom with her cup of coffee, she found Martha and Ann sitting on the bed. "I see JT slept with your slippers again. Why don't you just get another pair for you and give him these?" Martha said, pointing to where the soggy ones lay.

"Yeah, just put the new ones up on the shelf by your bed," Ann piped in.

"Have you noticed how tall he is? He could just reach up and pull them off the shelf. I have resigned myself to going barefoot; besides, I haven't the heart to take away his security blanket, so to speak."

Looking at JT and noticing the look in his eyes, Martha could see what Sophie was talking about. One look into those two pools of pitifulness was enough to make anyone do anything for him. "All right, I give, now quit giving me that look. Boy, do you know how to use those eyes to get what you want." She could swear that he was smiling at her, and when she looked into his thoughts, it was confirmed. "You're such a manipulator, but we love you anyway," Martha said, floating over and giving him a hug.

Ann giggled in the background. "He certainly has us wrapped around his large paws."

"Well, I don't know about you two, but JT and I are going shopping before our clients get here," Sophie said, pulling an old pair of jeans and empire waist shirt from the dresser. Getting dressed, she pulled a couple of bracelets and rings out of her jewelry box. Sliding the bracelets onto her wrist and rings onto her fingers, she looked at her reflection in the mirror. What she saw was a young woman with long, curly, auburn hair, pale face and round figure. What she didn't see was the fact that her topaz eyes held a wisdom far beyond her years, and although she was short, her figure was ample without being overweight.

"How I wish I were tall and thin with gorgeous blonde hair," she said, sighing deeply. "Oh well, you love me anyway, don't you, old man?" she asked the large pit bull at her side. He mooed agreement at her and leaned against her leg, nearly knocking her over.

Grabbing her purse from the kitchen table, she headed down the back stairs with JT close on her heels. Her late model GMC SUV was parked just outside the back yard fence. Unlocking it remotely, she opened the driver's side back door. She had just finished making sure the seat cover was in place when JT jumped into it.

"Well, just make yourself at home, why don't you," she mumbled, watching as he made himself comfortable on the seat. He took up the whole back seat with no extra room to spare. Planting her hands on her hips, she told him, "It's a good thing you didn't get any bigger, or I would have had to go to the full size." He just gave her a doggie grin, and she could hear him saying, "This is just the right size for me, Mom."

Laughing, she got into the driver's seat and headed for the local natural foods market. She felt JT nuzzle the back of her neck and knew he wanted the window down. Unlocking the parental override for the back window, she heard the window slide down and smiled to herself. She always believed him to be very intelligent, so she began teaching him as a puppy how to do things for himself. She taught him how to use his paw to open and close the window for himself. This was just one of many things she had taught him to do.

Arriving at the market, she instructed JT to watch the car, not that she would expect anyone to come close enough to bother it once they saw him in the car. She finished her shopping and loaded the groceries into the rear of the vehicle. Putting the grocery cart back in the cart corral, she got in the car and headed home.

Parking the car at the back of the house and unloaded the groceries. After putting them away, she headed to her office at the front of the house. The answering machine light was blinking, and she sat down at the desk to listen to her messages. There were several messages requesting appointments, and a call from her aunt with an invitation to the opera. Her aunt was the president of the opera guild and moved in very influential circles. Some of her best clients were referred to her by her aunt.

Making a note of the names and numbers left on the answering machine, she dialed her Aunt Toni's number.

She answered on the third ring. "Hello, Sophie, how are you and my favorite dog doing?"

Smiling at the sound of her aunt's voice, she answered, "We're great, Toni, and JT says hello."

"You give that big guy of yours a big kiss and hug for me. Well, are you going to go with me to the opera? They're doing La Boheme, and it's sold out. I know it's your favorite, and you're just lucky enough to have an aunt who can get you front row seats. Its Friday night; I'll pick you up at 6:30, and we can have dinner before we go. I'll bring Teddy over to keep JT company. Dan's away on a business trip; otherwise, I'd just have you bring JT to our house. They'll have a great time playing together."

"All right, you know of course they will leave nothing untouched in the house. I'll try to Teddy-proof the house as much as I can." Sophie laughed, remembering the last time JT and the little long haired wiener dog had the house to themselves. There wasn't a blanket, pillow, couch or bed left untouched by their joyous playing. For being such a little dog, Teddy certainly had energy in spades.

Hanging up the phone, she returned her calls and scheduled the readings. She was already booked out 3 months in advance. The rest of the week passed in a haze of clients and customers who all seemed to be looking for something special for someone.

Early Thursday morning, Sophie was busy doing the inventory before she opened the shop when the phone rang. Reaching for the phone, she noticed it was Brittany's number.

"So did you get the approval to pick up Zeus Saturday?"

"Absolutely, we can pick him up in the afternoon like we planned."

"Perfect, I can hardly wait to meet him. Do you have any more sculptures done for me?"

"Yes, I have several small figurines and a couple of medium sculptures ready to go. I'm also working on another large project like the last one you sold for me. It's going to be a sculpture of an angelic dog. I want to bring awareness of the plight of the pit bull, so I'm using JT as inspiration."

Hanging up the phone, she smiled to herself in anticipation of seeing the look on Bree's face when she finally picked up Zeus. Feeling a cold nose nuzzle her hand, she looked down to find JT standing next to her. "Yes, you're going to get to go when we pick up Zeus. I know you'll both be great friends. Now, we had better open the shop."

Friday morning dawned bright and beautiful. Stretching, Nick sat up on the side of the bed and noticed a coffee cup sitting on his night stand. He didn't remember putting it there. Picking up the mug, he noticed that it was his father's cup. It was the same cup Juanita had told him she found out on the counter every morning.

"Well, I'll be damned," he muttered to himself.

"Dad, I hope you're here, because if you're not, there are some of the strangest things going on around here."

Placing the cup back on the nightstand, he closed his eyes and was silent for several minutes. Hearing nothing, he opened his eyes to find that the mug was gone. "Wow!" Hearing Max whine, he turned his head to see the dog sitting in the bedroom doorway, staring out in the direction of the kitchen.

"What is it, Max? Do you see Dad?"

Max whined again and looked back in the direction of the kitchen.

"Max, find Dad," Nick said, getting up and following the dog.

Max headed for the kitchen and sat down directly in front of the coffee pot, looking over at Nick as if to say, 'He's right here.' There on the counter beside the coffee pot was his dad's coffee cup. Grinning from ear to ear, he rubbed Max's ears, saying, "Good boy, Max. Can you see Dad? I'm beginning to think that you really are seeing him. Dogs must be more sensitive to spirits than people are."

Picking up the coffee mug, it felt cold, as if it had just come out of the refrigerator.

"I think I need to talk to Mom about this boy. And I think I need to do a little research into ghosts. If I didn't have to go to the opera tonight, I would come home early and do it. But unfortunately, I've got a busy day today with two new clients. I have to go to the opera, because all the proceeds go to pet rescue, and that's worth putting up with Pamela at least one more time."

Setting up the coffee pot, he turned it on and let Max out into the back yard. Heading for the bedroom, he got into his running clothes. Once dressed, he headed for the back door, grabbing Max's leash as he went out.

"Come on, Max, let's get going."

Max didn't need to be told a second time; he ran over and sat down in front of Nick, whining excitedly. Heading out for their run, Nick's mind was still pondering the events of the morning. Returning to the house, he fed Max and jumped in the shower. Getting ready for work, he threw on jeans, boots and a short sleeve shirt. Heading back into the kitchen where his laptop was set up, he turned it on and grabbed a cup of coffee. Going through his email, he paid a few bills and saved a few to address later. Logging onto his work account email, he forwarded the ones that looked to be requests for job quotes to Adele so she could schedule appointments for them. By the time he finished, it was 7:30, and time to head to the office.

"Well, Max, are you ready to go?" Opening the door leading to the garage, Max needed no second invitation to head straight for the pickup. Opening the passenger side door, the dog jumped in and sat in the passenger seat. Smiling, Nick moved to the driver side and climbed in. Pushing the remote for the garage door, Nick backed his truck out and headed for the office.

Arriving at the office, Max followed Nick inside the back door. Adele's voice sounded from the front of the office, "Morning, Nick, is that Max I hear with you?"

"Good morning, Adele. Yes, I brought Max with me."

"Do I take it you're going to spend most of your day out in the field?"

"Yup, so whatever you have for me, we need to get through it before I head out," Nick said, stopping by Adele's desk.

"Hello, Max," Adele said, rubbing the dog's ears. "All right, go ahead into your office, and I'll get the things together that I need to discuss with you."

"Okay, did Max's bed get cleaned? I asked them to come in earlier in the week to clean it."

"Absolutely, you know Max is one of their favorite clients. They would make sure that it got done, no matter what."

"Yeah, one look in those big brown eyes is enough to melt most hearts," he said, grinning. Entering his office, he turned on his computer and sat down and went through some of the papers Adele had already placed on his desk.

Adele came in carrying a stack of papers and her appointment book. "I got the emails that you sent me, and I'll set up the appointment times for them. What days do you want to do these on? You have time on Tuesday, Wednesday, and Thursday of next week. You want to do morning or afternoon?"

"Those days are fine, and let's do afternoon; that way, I can get caught up on the paperwork and get started on the new apartment complex remodeling. Also, I wanted to let you know that I asked Jason to be the new project foreman. What he doesn't know is that I'm going to make him project director. I'm just waiting for him to give me his decision."

"I don't see why he even has to think about it, I'm sure he'll take the job."

"Yes, I'm sure he'll take the job, but I want to give him the opportunity to discuss it with Brenda."

"I agree, now that their first baby has been born, it's important to include Brenda in the decision."

"All right, what have you got for me this morning?"

Laying down a stack of papers in front of him, she said, "These just need your signature, and they're ready to go."

Signing the stack of papers, he handed them back to her.

"Here's the names and addresses for your two appointments today with new clients. The first appointment is at 11:30; they're looking to renovate an office building. The second client appointment is at 2:00. They're looking to renovate a two-story apartment complex."

"Thanks, Adele, I'll be leaving here in an hour. I've got a few call phone calls to make, then I'll be heading out."

"Okay, if there's anything important, I'll text it to you. Oh, and by the way, Pamela called this morning and said I was to remind you about the opera tonight. Are you about ready to give her the boot? She's driving me crazy and becoming really annoying."

Grinning at her, he said, "Yeah, she's beginning to get a little too possessive, and you know I can't stand the clingy type."

"Yeah, I know. Most of the other ones I could tolerate, but this one just rubs me the wrong way. Whenever she calls, she treats me like I'm a servant or something."

"I'm sorry about that, Adele. Hopefully, you won't have to deal with her anymore after tonight."

"It's too bad you can't get out of going to the opera tonight. I know you're only going because it benefits the local rescues, I just hope she doesn't make your evening miserable. If I were you, I'd wait till you drop her off to tell her you're not seeing her anymore."

Grinning wryly, he said, "That's what I'm going to do."

Heading back to her desk, she couldn't help but wish that she could be a fly on the wall when he told Pamela he was done with her. *Oh man, was she going to be pissed off. Just the thought of Pamela's reaction made her smile. His mom would certainly be glad that their relationship was over,* she thought.

An hour later, Nick and Max headed out the back door. "I'm leaving now, Adele, I'll see you Monday morning."

"Have a great weekend, Nick."

Nick spent the next six hours visiting work sites and giving new customer quotes. A little after four, he headed back to his house. He had around an hour and a half to get ready before he had to pick Pamela up. He was not looking forward to the confrontation with Pamela when he dropped her off tonight.

While Nick was busy getting ready for the evening, his guides were busy discussing the new turn of events.

"I am so glad he's getting rid of that woman, she's nothing but a thorn in my side," Helen remarked.

"I agree wholeheartedly with you, luv, she reminds me of a female barracuda. Not the kind you want to be cuddling up with, too many teeth," Sid said, grinning.

"All right, you two, that is enough of that. I'm sure she has some redeeming qualities, although they're not readily apparent to me," Bert said, smiling at them.

The comment was so unlike him that they were both stunned into silence for a moment. Then everyone started laughing at the same time.

"Bert, are we set for tonight?" he heard Martha ask in a communication that only he could hear.

"It's all set, and everything has been put in motion," he replied.

"Thank you, my friend."

By the time Nick finished getting ready, it was almost 5 o'clock. Heading into the kitchen, he opened the refrigerator and grabbed a large container with Max's name on it. Juanita always made up Max's dinner of meat rice and vegetables for a week at a time. Getting a bowl out of the cupboard, he put a portion of the mixture into it and put it in the microwave to heat for him. As the microwave slowly heated the mixture, Max set down in front of his eating mat. The timer went off on the microwave, and Nick pulled out the mixture, grabbing a spoon to stir it with.

"I can see you're hungry, and this smells good enough for me to eat. Juanita certainly spoils you, that's for sure. Here you go, big guy, at least you'll have a peaceful evening, which is more than I can say for myself," Nick said, sitting down the food on the mat.

The dog looked up at him, as if asking permission, and Nick said, "Take it."

Chapter 7

Friday flew by, and it was time to close the shop and get ready for the opera. Locking up the shop, she let JT outside and headed upstairs to get ready. Taking a quick shower, she headed back downstairs to let JT back in.

Entering the kitchen, she reheated the rice, vegetable and meat mixture she had made yesterday for him. "Well, big man, your favorite buddy is coming over to play with you tonight. Please try not to trash the bed too badly," she told him.

Leaving him to finish his dinner, she headed back to the bedroom to find something suitable to wear. Picking out two dresses and a skirt and blouse, she laid them on the bed, trying to decide which one to choose.

"I'd choose the black dress, you can never go wrong with a little black dress," Martha intoned.

"I agree, and it flows really well. That crystal necklace Bree made for you last Christmas would look great with the dress," Ann said.

"I would feel more comfortable in the suit, but since you both want me to wear the dress, I'll bow to your judgment." she told them. Laying the black dress across the chair, she hung up the other outfits.

After taking a shower, she sat down at her vanity and applied her makeup. By the time she finished, JT had made himself at home on the bed next to where Martha and Ann sat. "Well, don't you three look comfortable?" she said, smiling at them.

"Yes, we're quite comfortable, thank you." Martha said, rubbing JT's ears softly.

Shaking her head and smiling at them, she put on her panties and bra and slipped into a pair of shimmering pantyhose. Walking over to where the dress lay, she picked it up and slipped it over her head. The simple black dress was made of a shimmering material that hugged her body softly and flowed smoothly as she turned.

"It doesn't look too bad, I guess," she told them.

"Are you kidding? It's fabulous," Ann said. "It's got just the right amount of cling to hug your figure without being skin tight."

"Yes, dear, it's simple, but elegant. Now put on the necklace, and why don't you wear the crystal charm bracelet with it?" Martha suggested.

"All right, you two, this is a simple opera date with Toni, not a hot date with a guy," she said, rolling her eyes at them.

"You never know who you might run into at one of these functions," Ann said. Martha sent her a look that said 'Keep quiet' behind Sophie's back.

"They only people I've run into have been old enough to be my grandpa," Sophie said, rummaging through her jewelry box. Finding the necklace and the bracelet, she slipped them on and stood back to look in the mirror. "It does look rather elegant, doesn't it? It'll make a nice change from my usual jeans and tops. It feels nice against my skin." Twirling around, she asked JT, "What do you think? Do you like my new look?"

"If you like it, I like it," he relayed telepathically. She could tell that he was just being nice, he hadn't a clue sometimes about humans. She laughed and reached down to hug him.

"Better find your shoes, Toni will be here in a few minutes," Martha reminded her.

Looking at her watch, she noticed Martha was right, she only had about ten minutes before her aunt got there. Digging in her closet, she found her one and only pair of heels. The black patent leather shoes had 3-inch stiletto heels with rounded toes. Dusting them off, she slipped them on her feet and practiced walking around the room.

"Do be careful, we don't want you falling off your heels and injuring yourself," Martha said, smiling.

"Ha ha, very funny. That's why I'm practicing, so I won't fall and make a fool of myself and embarrass Toni."

She heard a car door slam through the open window, and JT headed down the back stairs, barking excitedly. Opening the door, JT ran to meet the other dog as he came through the gate. The small dog took off running, with the large one chasing after him.

"It's amazing, talk about an odd couple, these two are certainly it," Toni said, laughing.

"I agree, but you have to understand they have no concept of size, so to them they're both the same size. They don't care what the other dog looks like; it's all about energy and the intent of the other dog. I only wish people were the same, unfortunately, we haven't risen above the need to judge by appearance."

"You're right about that. Dan was just saying last week how much he hates to go to these functions, because he feels like everyone is judging him by his clothes. If it was up to him, he'd go in a sweatshirt and jeans, not nine hundred dollar suits. He says it's bad enough that he has to go to work in them. As the president of a large company, he needs to maintain a certain image when he really doesn't care what they think of him, only that his product is good," Toni said with a longsuffering sigh.

"Come on in, and we'll get these two guys settled for the evening."

Climbing the stairs to the second floor living space, Toni was once again struck by an overwhelming sense of peace and serenity that emanated from the cottage. It was the kind of place where you could relax and the stresses of the day would just melt away.

"I always love coming here, Sophie. It so reminds me of Mom, I'm glad you decided to keep the cottage after she died."

"Yes, it was a blessing that she made preparations for just such an event, but then I think she knew she was going to cross soon."

"I agree, she always seemed to be one step ahead of everything. You were lucky to inherit her abilities, your mother and I didn't inherit her gifts. But then I don't think your mother could have dealt with them, she's always been mentally unstable." She sighed, remembering the suicide of her younger sister.

"JT, come sit down, you too, Teddy," Sophie called them telepathically.

The dogs came running and plopped their bottoms down on the floor in front of her.

"Now, you two need to make sure you don't tip over the furniture, I don't mind about the rugs and the bed, but no tipping over the furniture," she warned them. Their tails wagged faster and faster as she communicated with them. "Don't give me that innocent look; you know what happened last time, little man," she said out loud, looking directly at the little dog. He turned his head to give his mistress a pitiful look.

She broke out laughing. "Wow, if that look got any more pathetic, he'd win an Oscar. You behave yourself, little man," she said, wagging her finger at him, "and I'll bring you back a treat. We'd better get going."

Picking up her purse, Sophie followed her aunt down the stairs, locking the door on her way out. She climbed into the passenger side of the low slung BMW sports coupe. "Love your new wheels, wish I could afford one of these," she said, admiring the plush leather interior of the vehicle. "But unfortunately, JT would be hard pressed to fit into the front passenger seat, let alone the back seat."

"Fortunately, Teddy is only king-size in personality," Toni said, laughing. Starting up the car, she turned it around. Leaving the driveway, she headed for the freeway entrance. "What are you up to this weekend, more clients?"

"Yes, Saturday morning is full, but I'm closing early. I have to take Bree to pick up her service dog Saturday afternoon. Sunday, I've got to do some housework and I'm having dinner with one of my clients."

"Male, I hope?"

"Unfortunately, no; it's an older woman, and she's very sweet. I helped her connect with her husband and find something that he hid away for her."

"I could always fix you up with one of Dan's friends, if you wanted."

Heaving a longsuffering sigh, she said, "No, thank you, that's quite all right, I don't have a problem with my own company. Not that I'm ever really alone, there are always plenty of souls who need help crossing over or communicating with a loved one."

"You need to talk to your guides and have them help you find someone nice. You're not getting any younger," she said with an exaggerated frown.

They both burst out laughing at the thought of 25 being considered old. When she could stop laughing, she commented, "You know, Grandma would have been the first to advise me to stay single and sow my wild oats."

"Yeah, that was dear old Mom. After Dad died, I'm not surprised that she never remarried. She always said there could never be another love for her like Dad."

They were both silent, deep in thoughts of the past.

Pulling up in front of the Heathman Hotel, they left the car in the capable hands of the valet and went inside for an early dinner. They were seated immediately in a small, cozy table.

Looking at the menu, she felt the hairs on the back of her neck stand up. She usually had this feeling just before something unexpectedly life-changing happened. Cautiously looking around from behind her menu, she couldn't see or sense anything unusual at the moment. Shrugging her shoulders, she tried to shake off the feeling and turned her attention back to the menu.

"So what are you going to have, Sophie? I think I'll have the seafood salad."

"I think I'll have the London broil, that way I can give the pups a treat, like I promised, if they were good."

"Are you kidding? You'll give it to them anyway. They certainly have your number," she said, laughing.

Sophie thought about it for a moment and grinned. "Yeah, they know a soft touch when they see one."

After placing their order, conversation turned to talk of Dan's upcoming surprise party and how they were going to pull it off.

"We have two weeks to get this party setup. I don't want to have the party at the house or any of our usual haunts, so I'm open to suggestions."

"After you told me what you wanted to do, I thought about it a lot, and I think I've found the perfect place for the party."

"Really, where?"

"It's a rather secluded place called the Stone Cliff Inn. It's located on the Clackamas River, out by Carver. It's a huge log cabin that they've turned into a restaurant. They have a lot of weddings, anniversaries and celebrations of all kinds there. You remember that vampire movie they came out with a few years ago?"

"Oh yeah, the same one I had to drag you to because Dan wouldn't go with me to see it. You mean some of the scenes were shot there?" she said, sounding excited.

"Yeah, one and the same. It's large enough to hold all his friends, without being so big you would lose him in a crowd. When you get home tonight, take a look at the website and see what you think."

"How marvelous, I'll do that and let you know tomorrow. I hope they're not all booked up."

"I have a feeling you'll be able to book the party, Martha says it shouldn't be a problem," she said, grinning secretively at Toni.

"Thank you, Martha."

"Martha says not to thank her, Grandma had something to do with it."

"Thanks, Mom."

Just then, the dinner arrived and conversation ceased.

"I can hardly stand the suspense. I wish they'd hurry up and eat so we can get to the Keller for the opera," Ann said excitedly to Martha.

"Contain yourself, child, everything happens when and where it's supposed to. Trying to hurry things along will not help it to happen any sooner. In fact, it may cause unforeseen complications," Martha warned.

Finishing their dinner, Sophie and Toni headed outside and walked the two blocks to the auditorium. Having season tickets and being guild members, they didn't have to wait in line.

Chapter 8

Nick grabbed his jacket and headed for the door to the garage. Bypassing his truck, he got into the Chrysler 300. Backing out of the driveway, he headed for Pamela's home in the West Hills. Pulling up into the driveway, he got out and went to the front door. He was about to ring the bell when the door opened and Pamela stood in the doorway. Reaching out for him, she gave him a big hug and a lingering kiss.

"You look marvelous, dear, but we better get going, or we'll be late for dinner. I made 5:30 dinner reservations for the Porto Terra restaurant at the Hilton for us. We'll have to hurry to get there on time," Pamela admonished.

Taking her by the arm, he walked her to the passenger side of his car and opened the door for her to get in. Once she was in, he closed the door and headed for the driver side.

Arriving at the Hilton with a few minutes to spare, they were seated in the restaurant right away. After having placed their order, Pamela started talking about her week. Nick only half-listened and gave the appropriate answers when needed. *There was nothing more boring than listening to Pamela talking about her charities and tearing people and things apart. Her conversation just reinforced his growing discontent with their relationship. The physical relationship between them had been great, but in the last couple of weeks, even that had been lacking,* he thought.

"This will be the perfect opportunity for you to meet other influential people who are also supporting the animal rescues. My aunt's a big advocate for animal rescues of all kinds, and I'd really like you to meet her tonight."

"She sounds very nice. I look forward to meeting her."

Their dinner arrived, and Nick was glad to have the excuse not to talk and focus on his dinner. He ordered the T-bone steak, which was done to perfection. Checking his watch, Nick noticed that it was 6:30, and the opera began at 7:30.

"We'd better get going if we're going to be there at a reasonable time," Nick said, signaling for the waiter. The waiter appeared at his side. "I'd like to get this bone wrapped up to go with me for my dog."

"Certainly, sir, I'll get that done right away," the waiter said, taking the plate away.

The waiter returned in a matter of minutes with the wrapped bone and the check. Paying the check, they left the restaurant and headed outside, where his car was just being brought out front by the valet. Arriving at the Keller auditorium, the valet parked their car and they headed inside. Arriving in the foyer, they found it packed with people.

Small tables lined the inner walls of the foyer, each one representing a different animal rescue organization. Someone came over to talk to Pamela, and Nick headed straight for the rescue tables. Talking to each one of the representatives, he left his business card with each one of them. He offered to help them build new kennels and facilities if they needed them. He told them he would even supply the building materials and labor. Many of the organizations needed to have new shelters built or improved but were unable to afford the cost to have it done. He advised them to give his office a call and leave a message with his secretary regarding what they needed and who they were. He told them to make sure that they mentioned they were represented at the opera.

Feeling a hand on his shoulder, he turned to see Pamela frowning at him. "I brought you here to meet new clients, not new rescues." Taking his arm, she led him over to where a group of men were discussing future building projects.

"Henry, I'd like you to meet Nick Stavros, he's the owner of Stavros construction. Nick, this is Henry Bradshaw. Nick's company did the renovation on the Heathman Hotel."

"Good to meet you, young man, I remember your father Bill. He was an honest man and did great building and renovation work. I'm glad to hear that you're continuing his legacy. I'm going to be renovating some high-end condominiums that I have. They're situated right on the Willamette River. Think you might be interested in giving me a quote?"

"Of course, sir, I would certainly be interested in the job. I remember my father talking about you and how much he enjoyed working for you."

"Well, boy, here's my card. You stop by my office Monday morning, and we'll talk about it," he said, handing Nick his business card. After that, the conversation turned to economics.

Pamela whispered in his ear, "I'm going to look for my aunt. I'll be right back."

Nick nodded understanding and continued to listen to the discussion at hand.

Pamela made her way around the room, greeting friends and acquaintances, while at the same time looking for her aunt.

Entering the foyer, Toni was greeted by friends and colleagues. Since Toni brought her whenever Dan was out of town, she knew several people. A lot of the people she met tonight were actually clients of hers. Because a lot of the people were old money, they came to her seeking business advice from relatives on the other side. These souls were the ones who originally made the wealth in the first place.

"Sophie, how are you, dear?" a voice spoke from behind her.

She turned to see an older woman of around 70 smiling at her and holding out her hand. "How's that gorgeous young man of yours doing? I've got to find time to stop by and see him soon."

Taking her hand, she leaned in and gave her a hug. "Catherine, it's good to see you again. I heard you had a little bout with gout."

"Yes, unfortunately I get it every now and then, but it's better now. I want you to meet my niece, Pamela Benson."

Catherine looked past Sophie's shoulder, searching for her niece. Spotting her heading her way, she called her niece's name.

Pamela had reached the far end of the foyer when she heard her name called. Turning in the direction the voice had come from, she saw her aunt standing and talking to two women. The first one she recognized as Antoinette Boyer, the head of the

Opera Guild. She was unfamiliar with the other younger woman. Making her way over to her aunt, she gave her a kiss on the cheek.

Sophie turned her head, looking over shoulder to see a tall, thin blonde haired woman moving towards them. The woman kissed her Catherine's cheek, smiling at her.

"Pamela, I'd like you to meet some friends of mine. This is Antoinette, a very dear friend and a member of the Opera Guild," she said, touching Toni's shoulder. "And this is her niece, Sophie."

"It's nice to meet you both," Pamela said with a phony smile on her face.

"It's very nice to meet you. Catherine has told me so much about you. It's nice to finally put a face with the name."

"Did you finally convince Nick to come with you tonight? I know he's not much of an opera fan, but I know he loves to sponsor animal rescue charities. And tonight is a really good one; there are several rescues that will benefit from tonight's proceeds," Catherine asked her.

"Yes, he's over there," she said, waving her hand in the direction of the far end of the foyer, where a group of men appeared to be talking animatedly. "I left them having a rather heated discussion about the cost of new construction."

"Why don't you bring him over and introduce him to Antoinette? She has a fondness for animal rights and rescue. And her niece Sophie here is an animal communicator and psychic medium. She donates a lot of time to the rescues to help troubled animals with behavioral problems."

"Really? How unusual," Pamela commented. "If you'll excuse me, I'll go and get Nick."

"Of course, what she really means is she hasn't a clue about or any belief in animal communication, let alone a psychic medium. Unfortunately, she is very narrow-minded. She must have gotten her genes from her father, because they certainly didn't come from my side of the family. We're all very open-minded about etheric issues."

"Not everyone is open, a lot of people have to see to believe. My father was like that, he believed if you can't touch it, feel it or see it, it doesn't exist, at least until he met my grandmother," Sophie said, grinning.

Walking back over to where Nick was deep in conversation with the other men, Pamela paused by his side. Waiting for a lull in the conversation, she interjected, "I hate to interrupt your conversation, gentlemen, but my aunt would like to meet Nick."

"By all means, Pamela, he should definitely meet Catherine," Henry said. "She's a real kick in the pants, Nick. Your father and her used to have fun arguing with each other about the cost of a project. Many a time, I had to step in the middle between the two of them, but it was all friendly disagreements. They always managed to work things out together. And besides, Catherine always did love a good bartering session."

Pamela took his arm and led him towards the far end of the foyer. It looked like she was headed for a group of three women. "Nick, I'd like you to meet my aunt, Catherine Spencer."

The older woman in the group facing him held out her hand to greet him. "Why, Nick, it's so good to finally meet you. Your father Bill and I used to have some rousing arguments when he worked for me. I knew he was right whenever he wanted to make a change to a project, but I always made him convince me anyway. If he hadn't been a married man, I would've snapped him up years ago," she said, laughing.

"Yeah, Dad did like a good argument; he wasn't Greek for nothing," Nick said, smiling at her.

"I'd like you to meet two friends of mine," she said, turning to the two other ladies with her.

The face of the man who was accompanying Pamela was one that had been haunting her dreams for the last week. It was the man who bought Bree's crystal sculpture. Sophie recognized him immediately.

For the first time, Nick really looked at the two women standing to the right of him. It was then that he noticed a familiar face. It was the woman with the haunting topaz eyes. He could hardly tear his eyes away from her face. He made himself concentrate on what Catherine was saying.

Sophie could tell that Nick was as surprised to see her as she was to see him.

"Nick Stavros, this is my best friend, Antoinette Boyer, and her niece, Sophie McGaughey."

"It's nice to meet you both," Nick said, acknowledging the women.

"You might be interested to know that Sophie is a psychic medium and an animal communicator. She donates a lot of her time to these rescues to help with behavioral issues."

"Mr. Stavros and I have met before," Sophie told Catherine. "He bought a very unique crystal sculpture Brittany created. He was looking for something unique for someone's birthday," she said, smiling at Pamela.

"Oh my," Katherine commented, turning her head to look at Pamela, "Brittany does exceptionally beautiful work. She's a genius when it comes to working with crystal. You really should go by Sophie's shop and look at some of the sculptures she's done. You can look it up online; it's called Outta Time, it's over in the Sellwood district. I know you don't generally frequent that area, but it would be well worth the drive. I'm one of her most frequent customers. Do you remember the sculpture I bought you last year for your birthday? It came from Sophie's shop. I remember you telling me how fascinated you were by the sculpture's ability to give the sculpture life."

"Yes, it's a fascinating sculpture." Pamela noticed how Nick's eyes kept returning to Sophie, as if he was fascinated by her.

Nick couldn't seem to stop himself from staring at Sophie. He could tell by her reaction that Pamela had noticed it, too. "*Crap*," Nick thought, "*it's not going to be a fun ride home tonight.*"

"Oh, it looks like people are beginning to take their seats; we had better go and find ours." Grabbing his arm, she pulled him in the direction of the auditorium. Finding their seats, they settled down to watch the opera. He found it hard to concentrate on the play, because he was constantly seeing Sophie's face in his mind's eye.

"Oh my, as much as I love Pamela, I have to admit, she has a temper like a shrew. I have the feeling that Nick's ride home is not going to be very comfortable," Catherine said, grinning at Sophie and Antoinette.

"If you ask me, that woman should have been spanked more as a child, and maybe she wouldn't be such a bitch," Antoinette chimed in.

"You're definitely right about that; my sister and brother-in-law indulged her from the moment she was born, which was a big mistake. I don't think she'll ever truly be happy, and my poor sister won't see any grandchildren either. Oh well, I'd really hate to think about what her children would be like if she did have any."

"She'll never be happy, because no one will ever be as perfect as she needs them to be," Sophie commented.

"I agree, she'll end up old and alone. Now that the rush for seats is over, let's go in and find ours," Catherine suggested.

They made their way down to the front row, where their seats were located. They were seated just in time for the curtains to go up on the show. They spent the next two hours lost in the magical world of La Boheme. Standing excitedly for the final curtain call, Sophie felt a rush of excitement.

Out in the foyer, two sets of guides were discussing the recent events.

"Well, I feel that went well, wouldn't you say, Martha?" Bert asked.

"I agree, it could have gone a lot worse; thank goodness for the power of surprise."

"I'm telling you, that bloke has not been able to get Sophie's eyes out of his head for the past week," Sid pointed out.

"Sid's right, you know, he's been spending an inordinate amount of time thinking about the color of her eyes. I would say he's obsessed by her, which is strange for him, and he doesn't like it. No woman has ever held such sway over his thoughts," Helen said, grinning.

"Well, Sophie's been thinking a lot about him, too. I think they're perfect for each other; if only we could get them both to see that," Ann said.

"I think they belong together, too, and I'll do everything I can to help. And besides, it's time for him to settle down," Bill spoke up.

Holding out her hand to Bill, she introduced herself. "Hello, I'm Martha, and this," she said, waving a hand in Ann's direction, "is Ann. She's a guide in training. We're Sophie's guardians. You must be Bill, Nick's father."

"Yes, ma'am." He held out his hand to her. "It's good to meet you. She's a wonderful girl; that's why I chose to send my message to her."

"Of course, we have to agree with you," she said, laughing.

"All right, everyone, let's go inside the auditorium with the others and listen to some beautiful music. After all, we're going to be here for another two hours."

"Bit long hair for me, luv, but I'm game if you are," Sid said. Smiling at Ann, he took her by the hand and they walked through the wall together.

The rest of them followed suit, and everyone took a seat high above the crowds. They spent the next two hours enjoying the opera. When the opera finished, people started filtering out of the auditorium.

Chapter 9

Nick knew he was in for the third degree when Pamela didn't stop to talk to any of her cronies on the way out. It seemed like everything was conspiring against him tonight. All he wanted to do was get rid of Pamela as quickly as possible, but somehow he knew it wouldn't be that easy. Sliding into the driver seat of his car, he headed towards Pamela's house. He didn't get more than a couple of blocks before Pamela started grilling him.

"So, that young woman said you bought a birthday gift for someone. I thought your mother's birthday wasn't until November?"

"It's not," he said without elaborating.

"Well, whose birthday did you buy it for? I highly doubt that Matthew would like something like that."

"Why is it so important for you to know who I bought the sculpture for?"

"Darling, I'm always interested in everything you do, you know that. I always try to take an interest in your family; after all, I am your significant other," she said, smiling sweetly at him.

"If you're really interested in who I bought the figurine for, I'll tell you. My mother told me about the sculpture, and she wanted to buy something for Sophie. So I bought the sculpture for her to give to Sophie."

"Why would your mother want to buy that woman a birthday present? I've never heard her mention this woman before. Come to think of it, I've never heard my aunt Catherine talk about her either. Just who is she?"

He could tell that curiosity was eating her up inside. He knew that he wasn't going to be the only one to get the third degree about tonight. He felt sorry for Catherine, but then again he smiled to himself; Catherine could give as good as she got.

"Most of what I know about her is from what your aunt Catherine told me tonight. She owns a crystal shop, and I believe she's a psychic medium and animal communicator as well. Not that I know much about that sort of thing. But I do know good craftsmanship, and the sculpture I bought was worth every penny. If it makes my mother smile, I would've paid twice the money."

Pamela suddenly realized that she may have pushed him a bit too far. When it came to his mother, she could do no wrong. "Yes, of course your mother's a wonderful person, and I agree she should have the best. Maybe I should drop by Sophie's shop to see if I can find something for my aunt's birthday. She seems to be absolutely enthralled by this woman's sculptures."

He realized it was only a couple of blocks until they arrived at her house. "Yes, she does seem to like them; maybe you should drop into the shop and see what you can find for her."

"Would you like to come in for a while? I just purchased some new black satin sheets; we can try them out."

At first he was going to turn her down, then he changed his mind. He couldn't stop thinking about Sophie and was hoping that a night with Pamela might get her out of his mind. "That sounds like a good idea," he said.

Once inside the door, they headed straight for the bedroom. They paused only long enough to peel their clothes off. Nick tossed Pamela down on the bed, and she let out a squeal. His lovemaking had a frantic quality to it. He was more aggressive in his lovemaking than he had ever been before with Pamela. She seemed to notice his aggression but put it down to sexual frustration.

As the night wore on, he tried repeatedly to wipe Sophie's image from his mind, each time without success. Around 2 am, Nick decided it was time to go home and left Pamela sleeping in her bed. Locking the door behind him, he climbed into the car and headed for home.

"Is he delusional or what? I'm telling you, I will never understand some men. He thinks that by having sex with one woman, he can completely cure himself of his obsession for another woman!" Helen told Bert.

"She was certainly pissed off that he was repeatedly looking at Sophie. I'll tell you something, luv, as a man, I can tell you Pamela has a nice body. But that's as far as that goes; what's on the inside is nothing but ice. The only fire she has is her anger and jealousy. I really feel sorry for her guides; it must be pure hell to work with her," Sid said with feeling.

"I'll tell you one thing, she has not forgotten him looking at Sophie for one moment. She's gonna latch onto this like a dog with a bone, and there's going to be hell to pay," Helen agreed.

"I would have to agree with you both, as you say, there's going to be hell to pay," Bert concurred.

Arriving at his house, Nick parked the car, turned off the alarm and headed inside. Max was there waiting for him, wiggling and whining. Squatting down in front of the dog, he hugged him and rubbed his ears. "Well, let's get you outside, young man, I've brought you a goody."

Letting the dog out the back door, he headed for the bedroom to get ready for bed. Hanging up his suit, he headed for the back door to let the dog in. Opening the door, Max hurried into the house and straight for the kitchen. Following behind him, he place the foil wrapped bone on the kitchen counter and slowly unwrapped it. Max sat down with a thud to wait for his goody.

"You knew I wouldn't forget you, didn't you, boy? Here it is, a nice, juicy T-bone just for you." He handed the bone to the dog, who took it gently from his hand and headed for his food mat. He stood for a minute and watched Max make short work of the bone.

"Boy, you are so lucky not to have to deal with dating someone. Pamela is becoming a thorn in my side. I don't know about you, boy, but after I shower, I'm headed for bed."

Chapter 10

"No matter how many times I watch this opera, it's like I'm watching it for the first time all over again. It's just so beautiful," Sophie commented.

"I agree, it's always a pleasure to see it performed in the traditional way. I always hate it when they try to modernize a classic opera. If it's a modern opera, then that's fine, but it changes the whole concept of the opera when they modernize it. Call me a stick in the mud if you want to, but I'm definitely a traditionalist when it comes to operas and stage plays," Antoinette said.

Heading towards the lobby, they said their goodbyes to the others and headed outside to await their turn in line for the valet to bring their car around. Once in the car, they spent the ride home talking about the play.

Arriving at Sophie's cottage, they pulled into the driveway and Sophie noticed Teddy looking out the window. "Take a look to your left in the second floor window," Sophie told her aunt.

"OMG, if I didn't know any better, I'd swear he was acting as a lookout," she said, laughing. "He's got to be standing on something, he's too short to look out the window like that. What do you think he's standing on?"

"I'd say he's standing on top of the glass table I have in front of the window. It's a good thing it's made sturdier than it looks, or it wouldn't hold up that little rascal."

Getting out of the car, she noticed Teddy must have jumped down, because he was no longer in the window. Unlocking the door, they headed upstairs to the apartment. Arriving in the living room, they found pillows everywhere, and the blankets that were used to cover the couch and chairs were on the floor, wadded up into a dog bed. Sophie and Antoinette gave each other a knowing look.

"Well, at least they didn't completely ransack the house. It sure looks like they had a great time." Placing her hands on her hips, Toni looked down at the long-haired Daschund. "Well, mister, you two must have worn yourselves out chasing each other and running around. You'll definitely sleep tonight, little man."

"I'd say they're both going to sleep like a stone tonight."

"So this is the first time that I've heard anything about your meeting Nick. Just when were you going to tell me about it?"

"Well, you know, it was kind of a funny thing."

"What do you mean 'kind of a funny thing'?"

"Have a seat, and I'll explain." They both sat down in the living room, and Sophie began to tell her what happened. "So it was a couple of weeks ago. I think it was Monday morning, and I was starting to do the inventory for the crystal. I heard a sound over by the door, so I looked towards the door and saw the handle turn, expecting someone to walk in. I heard the doorknob rattle, then someone knocked on the door. I went over to open the door, only it wouldn't budge. I've never had that door stick before. A man's voice from the other side told me that the door was sticking and he couldn't get in. He tells me to step back because he's going to put his shoulder against the door to try to open it. In the next instant, just as he's about to impact the door, it opens and he falls onto the floor at my feet."

"OMG, he didn't? You didn't laugh, did you? I know I certainly would have."

"No, somehow I managed not to laugh, but I did smile. He did look rather funny; such a big man lying there on the floor, and the door has never stuck before or since."

"Ah, I think it sounds like there was a little interference from the other side. What do you think?"

"I agree, not because I heard anything, mind you, but because his guides were conspicuously absent, at least they weren't showing themselves to me."

"So do you think it was his guides that made the door stick? And if so, why did they do it? Aren't they supposed to help you, not hinder you?"

"Well, you know if they think that you're going to do something that's not in your best interests, then they will try to keep you from doing it. Maybe he was in a bad mood, or maybe he was supposed to be somewhere else."

"Well, I for one would certainly like to know why they did it. One thing I did notice tonight is that he couldn't seem to take his eyes off you."

"I don't really think that he's interested in me, I'm not his type. That Pamela woman is more like his type, tall, blonde, skinny and beautiful."

"Wait just a minute, now there's nothing wrong with your figure. You're what's known as a full-figured woman. You have your curves in all the right places. You're not fat by any stretch of the imagination. Your grandma would have called you a womanly woman."

"Oh, well enough of that. I don't think I'm likely to see him anytime soon, so why worry about it? I'm kind of looking forward to having dinner with Jewel on Sunday, and so is JT. I'm going to take a bottle of wine that I think she'll like."

"Which one are you taking, the Moscato?"

"Yes, I'm taking the one made with pears and apples. Because as you know, there are several different types, and I've found this one to be the most flavorful."

"I agree, the Moscato would be just perfect for whatever she's fixing for dinner," Martha chimed in.

Sophie started laughing, and Toni asked, "What's so funny? No, don't tell me, it's got to be either Martha or Ann. I don't feel it's my guides. I may not know what they're saying, but I definitely know when they're talking to me. It's too bad I only got a little bit of Grandma's gift. There are times when I'd certainly like to know what they're saying and what they're up to."

"I really do think that you're blocking yourself. If you just let me help you open yourself up, you could hear what they're saying."

"I know, I know. Thanks for the offer; maybe when I get a little braver. Anyway, who said what?"

"That was Martha. She agrees that Moscato would be perfect for the dinner that Jewel is fixing." They both started laughing.

"Well, it's getting late. I'd better get this young man home to his bed. I've got a feeling that you'll see Nick again."

"Well, that's neither here nor there; I'll believe it when I see it." Giving her aunt a big hug, she scooped Teddy up and gave him a big hug and kiss. "Now you be a good boy for your mommy, and you can come over next week and play with JT." She handed the little dog to Toni.

Toni left, and Sophie headed to the bedroom. Removing her clothes, she gathered up her pajamas. Slipping into her bathrobe, she made her way into the bathroom for a shower. Finishing her shower, she slipped into her pajamas and told JT, "It's time to go to bed, big man. I think we both had enough excitement for one night."

Walking into the bedroom, she propped open the window to allow the warm summer breeze to blow through the bedroom. Pulling back the sheets, she climbed into the cool bed and was almost instantly asleep.

Saturday morning was spent in a flurry of clients and foot traffic customers. Before she knew it, it was time to close the shop and leave for Bree's house. Locking up the shop and house, she set the alarm and they headed for the car. They picked up Bree and headed towards the guide dogs for the blind in Sandy. It took them about 30 minutes to arrive at the center.

Arriving at the center, Sophie led Bree inside, where an older woman greeted her by name.

"Bree, good to see you again. Zeus has been waiting impatiently for you to get here. Let me go get him." She turned and disappeared through the door behind her. It couldn't have been more than a few minutes when she returned with a large fawn colored pit bull. "Let's go into the meeting room, where we can be comfortable." Handing Zeus's harness to Bree, she led her to the meeting room.

Sophie left them to talk and went back out to the car to take JT for a walk. By the time they returned from their walk, Bree and Zeus were ready to go. Squatting down beside Zeus, Sophie opened up her mind to the dog. Zeus was startled by the fact that he could understand what Sophie was telling him. Once the connection was established, she let him know if he had any questions or concerns, he could come to her for help.

The ride home was full of planning and excitement for Bree and Zeus. Dropping them off at their house, Sophie headed for home.

Pulling into the driveway, Sophie noticed that the weeds were starting to overtake her flower beds in the front yard. Looking at her watch, she realized she had a good three hours of light left in the day. Making a decision, she changed into some old clothes and headed outside to do some weeding while there was still enough light to see.

JT played happily in the yard while Sophie spent the next hour and a half weeding the flower beds. Pulling the last weed, she stood back to survey her handiwork. Not a weed in sight, and the flowers stood out brightly against the deep brown soil. Slipping off her gardening gloves, she put them on the back porch and went inside to get cleaned up.

Changing into her lounging pajamas, she went back downstairs and called JT in from the yard. He came running inside, not stopping until he had made it to the kitchen. Fixing herself and JT something for dinner, she sat down to eat and check her emails at the kitchen table. Finishing her dinner, she went into the living room and sat down on her recumbent bike to work out while she watched the evening news.

An hour later, she headed for the shower and changed into her pajamas.

"Time for bed, big guy, let's hit the sack." Climbing into the cool sheets, she drifted off to sleep.

Chapter 11

The early morning summer sun streamed in through the bedroom window, waking Sophie with its warm, golden glow. Yawning and stretching, she reached out to the other side of the bed and found JT's warm, furry body curled up in a ball. Looking over at the bedside clock, she realized it was 6 o'clock and the sun had been up for at least an hour. Rolling over to the other side of the bed, she gave JT a hug and said, "Come on, old man, it's time to get up; we're wasting daylight."

His only response was to groan and curl into an even tighter ball. "All right, you can stay in bed until I finish getting ready," she told him, smiling. Throwing on some jean shorts and a loose fitting thigh length top, she headed for the kitchen to make a cup of coffee. Walking over to the refrigerator, she pulled out a large square container full of three different types of meat. Every weekend, she cooked up fresh meat from the local butcher shop. She mixed some of the meat with the natural high-protein dog food that she buys for JT. She spooned out some meat into a separate bowl and put the rest back in the refrigerator. She microwaved the meat until it was warm, and then mixed it with the dry dog food. Just as she finished mixing the food, JT came wandering into the kitchen.

"Well, see how you are? You won't get up for me, but you'll certainly get up for food." He let out a big yawn and sat down, waiting for her to place the bowl on his feeding mat.

"I can certainly tell that you're in a couch potato mood today, but it's not going to happen because I've got a busy Sunday planned. We've got to go to the pet store, pick up gas, go to the post office and then stop by Jenna's shop. So if you want to ride shotgun with me, you'd better eat your breakfast and take a trip outside."

Grabbing her coffee, she headed into her office and turned on the computer to check her emails. 15 minutes later, she turned off her computer, grabbed her purse and keys, and headed for the door. JT, not wanting to miss an opportunity to go for a ride, was close behind her. Opening up the back door of the SUV, she placed her purse in the front seat and went back to the gate to let JT out. He automatically jumped in the back seat of the vehicle, ready to go for a ride.

Starting the car, they headed for Jenna's. Arriving at the shop, they both went inside and were greeted immediately by Jenna.

"Sophie, it's so good to see you, where have you been hiding yourself?"

"I know, I'm so sorry. I've been getting so many new clients that I'm booked through the next three months."

"Wow, that's great. I see you brought the young man along with you," she said, walking over to lean down and pet JT.

"Of course, I have to have my co-pilot with me. Once he knew where we were going, he could hardly contain his excitement. You'll never guess, a couple of weeks ago I sold Bree's big project."

"How wonderful, did you get full price for it?"

"I not only got full price, but I actually got $300 more."

"I'll bet Brittany was over the moon about it."

"Absolutely, it allowed her to be able to pick up her service dog, Zeus. They're doing really wonderful together, and their bond is sealed."

"So what can I get for you today?"

"I need 2 pounds of white Sage leaves, 10 pounds of Dead Sea salt, a pound of powdered charcoal, powdered Sandlewood and some sweet grass. I see you have some new jewelry, so while you're getting those things together, I'll just browse through the new pieces."

While Sophie looked at the new moon stone jewelry, JT made his way behind the counter, where the natural doggie treats were kept. Taking a treat carefully out of the bucket, he lay down to enjoy it. Jenna finished packing up the supplies, and Sophie met her at the counter with the Moonstone necklace that she had found.

"This is one of my favorite new pieces; I knew you might be interested in this particular piece," Jenna told her. The pendant on the necklace was a crescent moon with a round Moonstone hanging cupped by the crescent moon. Paying for her items, she said goodbye and they headed back out to the car.

They spent the next hour and a half finishing their shopping and headed back home. By the time they got home, it was 9:30. Taking the groceries and supplies into the house, she spent the next 15 minutes putting everything away. Heading downstairs, she got the shop ready for opening.

The next three hours were spent dealing with shoppers. She had just finished packaging up her last sale when the bell over the door sounded. She looked up to greet the new arrival and received a shock. Pamela walked in the door and started looking around. To say that she was surprised was an understatement. She walked over to where Pamela was looking at a large display of crystals.

"Hello, Pamela, it's nice to see you. Is there anything I can help you with?"

"I took my aunt's advice and decided to visit your shop. Her wedding anniversary is coming up, and since she seems to be enthralled with your crystal sculptures, I thought I'd see what was available."

"Are you looking for anything in particular? I do have something that I think Catherine would enjoy, but it's a little expensive."

Pamela sent her a condescending look and said, "When it comes to my aunt, nothing is too expensive. Why don't you be a good girl and bring out anything you think my aunt would like?"

Walking towards the back room, she heard Martha say telepathically, "I don't like that woman, she's got a hidden agenda; you just wait and see."

"I don't care if she's Lucretia Borja. If she buys one of Brittany's sculptures, then she's welcome here anytime."

"Well, I for one do not trust her," Martha told her.

Walking into the back room, Sophie headed for the tall old-fashioned safe set against the back wall. Opening the safe, she took out a box about the size of a shoebox. Closing the safe, she took the box back into the shop, where Pamela was waiting.

"If you follow me over to the table, we can open it up and I'll show you."

Walking over to the octagonal table, she opened the box and placed the 2 intricately crafted sculptures in the middle of the table. The figures were of two black and white Lhasa Apso dogs. The morning sunlight caught and was reflected in the crystal figurines.

"OMG, they are so beautiful. My aunt will love these," Pamela said as she picked up and examined each of the figurines. "They look exactly like my aunt's two dogs, Jack and Benny. I'll take them both."

"Would you like it gift wrapped?"

"No, just seal the box securely," Pamela said, following Sophie over to the cash register.

As Sophie began to wrap the pieces in bubble wrap, Pamela asked, "So how long have you and Jewel known each other? I've never heard her mention your name."

"I met her several months ago when she and her friend came to visit me for a reading, and we've been friends ever since."

"Nick and I have been together for a couple of years now, and I think he's about to ask me to marry him."

"Congratulations. I hope you'll both be very happy," Sophie told her, surprised at the jealousy and disappointment that filled her.

"Oh, we will be; we just need to set up the date. He wanted to wait a reasonable amount of time after his father died."

Sensing a change in his master, JT got up from his bed and came over to the cash register area. He walked over to where Pamela stood and woofed softly at her. Startled, Pamela turned to look at the dog and started backing up. "Is that thing going to attack me? Get that vicious creature away from me," she said, panicked.

"He's really quite gentle for his size," she told her. "*JT, come back over here. You don't want to go anywhere near her; she might bite you*," she told him telepathically. He looked startled and scampered back behind the counter.

"I don't care. I don't want him anywhere near me," she said emphatically.

"That will be $700, cash or credit?" Sophie asked her.

Pamela dug into her wallet and handed Sophie a $1000 bill. "You do have change, don't you?"

"Of course." Taking the thousand dollar bill from her, she returned $300, handing her the bag with the figurines. "Thank you for coming in today."

Watching Pamela leave the shop, she was glad she decided to close early today. She hadn't realized just how much the news of Pamela's engagement to Nick would affect her. She felt a wave of intense jealousy, followed by a sinking feeling in the pit of her stomach. Until that moment, she hadn't dared to analyze her feelings for Nick. Now she was forced to face her feelings and to admit that she was in love with him. She didn't understand how she could possibly be in love with him. She had only met him twice, yet she couldn't deny how she felt.

"Come on, Sophie, stop and think about it. Search deep inside you, what do you feel when you think of Nick?" Martha asked her.

Closing her eyes, she focused on an image of Nick, then of herself. She saw a type of umbilical cord stretching from herself to Nick. She knew this meant that she and Nick were soulmates. The thought had never occurred to her before this that she would meet her soulmate in this lifetime. Opening her eyes, she sat down, feeling like someone had just hit her in the stomach. She was struck by the irony of the situation. Here was a man who had no belief in her or her gifts. They were worlds apart, and he was already engaged to be married.

She felt JT nuzzle her arm, as if reminding her of the time. Looking at the clock, she realized she only had a few minutes before Brittany arrived. She heard the bell above the door ring, Brittany was early.

"Hey there, we're here," she heard Brittany call out as she opened the door.

"Hello, both of you."

"I've brought you some new figurines."

"Wonderful, I just sold another one of your large figurines," Sophie said.

Brittany and Zeus were standing next to the cash register, waiting for her. "So how are you and Zeus doing? It's a beautiful summer day, perfect for your walk over here." She walked over and ruffled Zeus' ears. "What have you brought for me?"

"I finished three of the larger figurines." Setting her case up on the counter, she unlocked and opened it. Reaching into the case, she pulled out three cloth covered objects.

Sophie opened the first wrapped object to find a crystalline statue of Zeus. The second object was of a cat playing with the ball of string. The third and final object appeared to be a vortex with a wraith-like figure emerging from it.

"These are absolutely marvelous. I should be able to sell them very quickly. In fact, I have a friend who runs a paranormal investigative team, and I think he would absolutely love to have the vortex figurine. I sold the dog set today. I managed to get $700 cash for it." Opening the cash register, she pulled out six $100 bills and handed them to her.

"Woo hoo, I'm so excited, I could dance. Now tell me about this new man in your life."

"How did…you know about Nick? Never mind, forget I even asked."

Laughing, Bree said, "I may be blind, but my psychic abilities help me to see what my eyes don't."

She told her about how she met Nick and their second meeting at the opera.

"Well, from what I can see, I think Nick is definitely interested in you."

"I might believe you, except for one thing, his fiancée was in here this morning. She's the one who bought the dog set. She let me know in no uncertain terms that they were engaged and were just waiting to set the date."

"Umm, I don't think everything is as it appears to be. The message I'm getting is something about an illusion. That's all they're giving me; the rest is for you to work out. Look, I gotta go, I have an appointment with the dentist today for a cleaning."

Walking her to the door, she flipped the open sign to close and headed over to the cash register to balance her ledger and put the money in a bank deposit pouch. Heading to the back room where the safe was located, she opened it and placed the bank envelope inside. She had just finished when there was a knock on the door. *That's odd,* she thought, *usually people don't knock when they see the closed sign.*

Chapter 12

Something wet and cold touching his arm startled Nick awake the next morning. Max stood next to the bed, wiggling his stub and looking excited. Reaching over, he stroked the dog's ears. "All right, all right I'm getting up to let you out."

The dog barked excitedly and headed for the back door, with Nick following close behind. Letting Max outside, he stopped in the kitchen long enough to put on a pot of coffee. Taking a quick shower, he got dressed and headed for the back door, where Max was waiting to come inside.

Letting the dog in, he headed back towards the kitchen to feed him. With Max fed, he turned on his laptop, poured himself a cup of coffee and sat down at the kitchen table to check his emails. He had just finished reading his emails when the telephone rang. Picking up the phone, he saw his mother's number on the Caller ID.

"Hi, Mom, what's up?"

"Hello, dear, how was the opera?"

"It was fine. They had a lot of rescue groups represented there, which was really great. I met Pamela's aunt, Catherine Spencer, last night."

"I remember your father used to do a lot of business with Catherine." She started laughing. "They used to fight like an old married couple over any kind of change in the plans for the projects. He knew she'd eventually come around to his way of thinking. It's my opinion she knew he was right but wanted to make him work for it. I believe that most people gave in to her easily, but your father was no yes man, and she liked that."

"Yeah, I kind of got that impression last night, and I really liked her. She's got a project she wants to talk to me about. I'm going to give her a call next week to set up a time to discuss her project. I also met Henry Bradshaw, he has a couple of projects he wants to discuss. Looks like I'm going to be busy."

"Sounds like Pamela's finally being useful. You know I don't usually say anything about the women you date. But I have to say that I really do not like Pamela, she puts on too many airs for me."

"I kind of guessed that, Mom, but you don't need to worry; I think I'm ready to be done with her. She's becoming entirely too possessive, and the spark that used to be there between us seems to have faded."

"Well, I'm glad to hear it. One of the reasons I called you was to let you know the lawyers have sold the stock and they're going to transfer half the money into the business account by the end the next week. I was able to get almost $2 million for the stocks. I'm going to give Matthew some of the money for his business, too."

"That's great, I hope you kept some of the money for yourself."

"Yes, dear, I kept enough to keep myself comfortable. The other thing I called about was to ask if you would come to dinner Sunday night at six. I invited someone I'd like both you and Matt to meet. She's become a good friend to me."

"Sure, Mom, do you want me to bring anything?"

"You might want to pick up some soft drinks. Why don't you bring Max with you?"

"Okay, Mom, we'll be there," he said, hanging up the phone.

He decided to fix himself some breakfast. He fried a couple of eggs, put some bread in the toaster and decided to add some bacon. Putting the bacon into the frying pan, he stood watching it cook, not really seeing the bacon. In its place he saw Sophie's face looking at him, full of amusement. The smoke detector suddenly went off, and he realized that his bacon was beginning to burn. Grabbing the frying pan, he removed it from the burner and turned off the stove.

Putting the food on the plate, he grabbed the toast that was almost cold, buttered it and carried it to the kitchen table. Pouring himself another cup of coffee, he sat down at the table to eat his breakfast.

"Well, Max, it looks like you're going to get a couple of pieces of bacon for breakfast."

The dog whined in anticipation and sat down next to the table to wait. Breaking a piece of bacon in half, he gave it to Max.

Once again, Sophie's face intruded into his thoughts and he remembered what his mother had said regarding Sophie. How she had helped her find the hidden panel where the stocks were located. She had never met his father or been to his mother's house, so far as he knew. And even if she had, what are the odds of her finding his father's hidden compartment when his own wife couldn't find it?

And then there were his own experiences at his home. He remembered as a small child his grandmother telling him when his grandfather died that death was not the end, but a beginning. He also remembered her talking to what she called 'spirit beings'.

"Bill, why don't you help Nick remember the time after his grandfather's death when he came to visit him?" Bert suggested.

"How do I do that?" he wanted to know.

"All you have to do is reach into his mind and mention his grandfather's death, and it will trigger the memory."

"All right, here goes."

Suddenly, a distant memory formed in his mind. He was a child of six years old, and his mother's father had just died. He was playing in his room, and he looked up to see his grandfather standing in the doorway. He noticed that he could see through his Grandpa, but he wasn't afraid; he was happy instead. His mother must have been wrong about Grandpa dying, because he was standing in his room. Grandpa smiled at him and told him that he was with Jesus and he was happy. He also told him that his grandma was right, that death was not the end, but a new beginning, and he was going to be watching over him. He remembered feeling happy that his grandfather would be watching over him. Running into the living room, he told his grandmother about Grandpa's visit. She gave him a big hug and let him know how special he was that Grandpa had come to him.

The more he thought about it, the more he was convinced that there was something to all of this. Maybe Sophie was the real thing, maybe his father really was trying to communicate with him. After all, there's no way that coffee cup could have moved all by itself. His curiosity was getting the better of him, so he decided to drop by her shop later that day.

He had several building projects going on and decided to stop by the sites to see how things were progressing. Grabbing his wallet, cell phone and Max's leash, he headed for the door.

"Come on, Max, let's go." He didn't have to ask twice, Max was already at the door.

Opening the passenger door, Max jumped in the truck. Climbing into the driver's seat, he punched the remote for the garage door and backed out of the garage. Closing the door, he headed for the site farthest away from him. Thirty minutes later, he pulled up in front of the site and opened the gate, driving the truck inside and closing the gates behind him. He opened the passenger door, slipping Max's leash on they headed inside the building. An hour and a half later, he finished his inspection and they headed on to the next site. Four hours later, he had finished visiting all the sites and decided to stop by Sophie's shop to see if he could talk to her.

He arrived at her shop around noon, just as a woman was coming out sporting a white cane. The dog was an unusual breed for a service dog, it was a pit bull. He waited for her to come down the walkway so that he wouldn't be in her way. She paused at the end of the walkway, tilted her head and said, "Hello, Nick, you've come at the perfect time. I think she needs to get some lunch. Why don't you take her out to lunch?" She urged him and continued walking away from him.

Nick was so startled by what the woman said that he was literally at a loss for words. Before he could recover, she was already at the end of the block.

It left him wondering how a woman who he assumed was blind and whom he had never met before knew his name. Meeting her had left him with more questions and no answers. Shaking his head as if to clear it, he walked up to the cottage. Seeing the closed sign, he knocked on the door.

Coming out of the back room, she was startled to see Nick standing at the door. He was the last person she expected to see again.

Opening the door, she asked, "What can I do for you, Mr. Stavros? Are you looking for another gift?" It was the only possible reason that she could think of for him to be coming to her shop again.

"Not this time, I would actually like to talk to you about something that happened to me, something I don't understand."

"I don't know what I could possibly help you with, as you don't believe in any of this mumbo-jumbo," she told him, smiling blandly.

"Yeah, I'm sorry about that. You know the old adage, I have to see it to believe it? Well, I've seen it, but I don't understand it. I need your help to understand it. Will you help me?"

She thought for a fleeting moment about telling him to take a hike but then thought better of it. Maybe, just maybe she could change his mind, and possibly his belief in the paranormal. She would sure give it a try. Maybe if he opened his mind, his father would be able to get through to him.

She stood looking at him, as if considering his request. She was silent for so long that he wasn't sure she was going to answer him.

"Have you eaten lunch yet? How about we go to lunch, my treat? Do you know of a good place around here to eat?" he asked, almost stumbling in his haste to get the words out. Afraid she might say no.

She surprised him by saying, "Let me lock up, there's a café a couple of doors down where we can get some lunch and you can tell me what's going on." She headed for the back room again. She reappeared with an oversized bag draped over her shoulder. Digging into her bag, she produced a set of keys. "Shall we go?" she asked him, heading for the door. "You might want to get Max and bring him along."

"Come on, JT, we're going to go visit Sheila at the café," she said, smiling at him.

Opening the door, she followed JT outside and locked the door. Sitting on the top step of the porch, JT waited for Sophie to finish locking up.

"Sure, let me get Max out of the truck," he said, heading out the door. Pausing in mid-stride, he wondered how she knew Max was in the truck. He hadn't heard him bark. Reaching the truck, he grabbed the leash out of the back and opened the passenger side, slipping the leash over Max's head.

He turned to find her waiting for him on the sidewalk. She turned to the left and started walking, the dog by her side. He noticed that she didn't use a leash, but the dog was never more than a step away from her. She stopped in front of a small café with outside tables two blocks away. The name of the café was the Hungry Dog. He grinned, thinking how appropriate it was. She pulled out a chair and sat down, and he did the same.

"I love this café, and so does JT. You can order for yourself and Max," she told him.

"How do you do that?" he wanted to know.

"Do what?"

"How did you know Max's name? And how did the blind woman who came out of your shop when I arrived know my name?"

She threw her head back, laughing, the sound was full-bodied and infectious. He found himself laughing, even though he didn't know what he was laughing about.

"I know Max's name because he told me what it was. And Brittany is a very powerful medium. She may be blind, but only in the physical sense of the word. She's the one who created the figurine you bought."

"This is just so strange to me. I feel completely out of my depth. I don't understand it, but I think I want and need to."

"Well, that's a step in the right direction. Unfortunately, a lot of people are very closed-minded."

Just then, the waitress came out, giving them menus and telling them the specials of the day. "Hello, Sophie. How are you doing, big man?" she greeted them both. Turning to Nick, she told him, "We have two menus; one for people, and one for your dogs." She left him to study the menus. It only took a few minutes for Nick to decide what he and Max would have for lunch.

The waitress returned, and they both ordered.

"Why don't you tell me what's been going on?" she invited him.

Taking a long drink of his iced tea, he set the glass down and began to explain.

"I came home a couple weeks ago and went downstairs to work out, as I always do after I get home. Max was acting strange, he was lying on his bed and was staring over at the futon with his ears perked up, like he was listening to someone or something. I dismissed it at first and got on the treadmill and finished my workout. I was wiping my face when there was a bang behind me. I turned and noticed a picture had fallen down on its face on the mantel."

"Max could have been hearing something outside and responding to it. The picture may have just fallen down from the vibration from your workout."

"You don't think I hadn't thought of that? Maybe Max did hear something outside, but it certainly looked to me like he was listening to someone. He had his head cocked to the side, and his ears were moving. As for the picture, granted, I agree it could have fallen over from the vibration of the treadmill. But the thing is, the picture wasn't supposed to be down there at all. It's a picture of myself and my dad. He died last year, and it was the last picture we had taken together. It's always kept in the bedroom on my nightstand. I live by myself, so I spoke to my housekeeper, and she has no idea how it got there. When I was talking to her, she also told me how every morning since my dad died, when she comes in to do the cleaning, she finds my dad's coffee cup sitting by the coffee pot. I had no idea that any of this was happening."

"So what else has happened?"

He shouldn't really be surprised she knew that there was more to it than he had already told her. "I started thinking about it, so I sat down and said, 'Dad, if you're here, do something to let me know'. I didn't hear or see anything, so I went to bed, and when I got up in the morning, my father's coffee cup was sitting on my nightstand."

"Well, it sounds like your father is trying to change your mind about life after death. He's trying to let you know that he is there and he is aware of what's going on in your life. As for Max, you need to understand that animals are much more open and sensitive to the other side than most humans. He was either seeing your father or your guides. If it had been something bad, Max would've started growling. They have an instinct about people and entities who may try to harm someone."

"So obviously, whoever he was seeing, he liked; is that what you're saying?"

"Yes, that's exactly what I'm saying."

"What are guides?"

"Guides are souls that have completely ascended to the other side, some people call it heaven. They are assigned to watch over us and help us during our physical lives."

Their lunch came just then, and they ate in silence. Finishing their lunch, Nick paid the check and they started walking back to her shop.

"Ask him about what happened when he was six, Sophie," Martha told her telepathically.

"There's something more you're not telling me; what happened when you were six?"

"Something odd happened this morning. I was sitting eating breakfast when suddenly I remembered something that happened when I was around six years old. My grandfather had just died, and I was in my room playing. I had a funny feeling, and I looked up and saw my grandpa there. I told him that I was glad he wasn't dead. He told me that he was dead but that he was okay and that he would be watching over me. He told me that Grandma was right, death is not the end, but the beginning. I haven't thought of that incident in years."

"It sounds like your father had a hand in helping you remember that particular incident."

"You mean they can do that? They can just pull a memory out of your brain and help you to remember it?"

"Yes, it happens all the time. Have you ever had a name pop into your head out of the blue or felt the urge to go somewhere or not go somewhere? This is usually those on the other side's trying to communicate with us. Another way they communicate is through dreams, because in the sleeping state our subconscious is open to receiving messages from them." Looking at her watch, she realized it was already 1:30. "I hope I was able to help clarify things for you. I'm sorry, but I have an appointment scheduled at 2:30, and I have to leave."

"Yes, you've helped me tremendously. How much do I owe you for your time?" he asked.

She felt like he just slapped her in the face. "Unlike your fiancée, not everything is all about money!"

He grabbed her by the arm to stop her from leaving, and JT growled at him, taking a step forward. He dropped her arm and said, "What are you talking about? I don't have a fiancée!"

"Well, that's not what Pamela said when she was in here earlier this morning. She was telling me that you're in the process of setting a date."

"What in the hell? I have not, nor have I ever been engaged to be married. I am not interested in getting married."

"Well, maybe you need to let Pamela know that," Sophie said.

"Sophie, I need to tell you something. The day I came into your shop, I was upset. I thought you were a fake and that you were milking my mother for money. I was wrong."

"I would never cheat anyone. I believe in the barter system, if a person doesn't have the money to pay me, then they can exchange goods or a service for the reading. I have a woman who has a small shop where she makes and sells homemade dog treats. If she needs advice, she'll bring me some dog treats for JT in exchange for my service."

"I'm very sorry that I prejudged you."

"I accept your apology. You're not the first, nor will you be the last person who doesn't understand or accept my gifts." Turning around, she headed into the shop, leaving Nick standing on the sidewalk.

Stepping inside the shop, she locked the door after herself. She headed for the back room and grabbed her mail cart. Heading out front with the cart, she picked up all of the expensive crystals, wrapped them in cloth and put them on the cart. She left the smaller pieces in the window display and took the more expensive ones and put them in the safe in the back room.

Heading upstairs, she changed into shorts and a tank top. Grabbing her purse and keys, she and JT left the house and headed down the block to the small salon located in the next block. Arriving at the salon, she and JT were greeted by Sylvia, the owner of the shop. She loves the shop and the people who work there. They were not only talented, but pet-friendly as well.

"Hey Sophie, you're right on time as usual. Sadie's been waiting to see JT all day," Sylvia said with a smile, referring to the bulldog sleeping in the corner of the pet area.

"JT, why don't you go over and wake Sadie up?" Sophie said.

He headed over and nuzzled the sleeping Sadie. She snorted and woke up. Seeing JT, she got up and started wiggling. The two of them began playing.

"Come on over and have a seat and tell me what you want to do today," Sylvia said.

"I need a trim and conditioner."

"Sure, no problem," she said, putting the drape around her neck and leading her over to the shampoo sink.

Chapter 13

Nick couldn't believe it, he couldn't believe that Pamela would come here and claim to be his fiancée. It seemed to him to be beyond comprehension. He had never given her any indication that he wanted a long-standing relationship with her. He was definitely going to have a conversation with her that she was not going to like. Heading for his truck, he opened the door for Max to jump in. Going around the front of the truck, he got into the driver's seat. He had a few errands to run before he could head home.

"Well, well, the cat's really out of the bag now," Helen said, smiling. "I am so going to enjoy watching him tell her off."

"Aren't we all, luv? We've got a front row seat, the only thing that's missing is a bowl of popcorn to watch the fight," Sid said, laughing.

"Since we don't eat, the popcorn would be wasted," Bert said with a smile. "I wonder where Bill's gotten off to."

"He's probably visiting Jewel," Helen said. "He likes to spend time with her."

"I thought that may have been the case. I'll call him; he's going to want to hear this."

"No need to call, I'm here. What's up?" Bill asked.

"He's about to dump the barracuda, and we've got a ringside seat!" Sid said, grinning from ear to ear.

"It's about darn time!" Bill said. "Let's go; I don't want to miss a moment of this."

They all disappeared and reappeared riding above the truck.

Pushing the button on his truck's radio, he was instantly connected to his cell phone. "Call New China." He was instantly connected to the restaurant. Placing his order, he swung by and picked it up on the way home. Arriving at the house, he let Max into the back yard and went to change his clothes.

Clothes changed, he headed to the back door to let Max in. "Let's go have some dinner, boy." Reaching into the refrigerator, he pulled out a container holding Max's food. Putting some of the food into another bowl, he heated it up in the microwave and transferred it to his dog bowl.

He suddenly noticed the light on the answering machine was blinking. Picking up the handset of the phone, he looked at the Caller ID. The first number was his mother's, and the other was Pamela's number. He decided to wait until after he finished dinner before calling his mother and Pamela back.

Sitting down at the kitchen table, he decided he wouldn't bother with plates and ate his meal straight out of the cartons. The more he thought about his visit with Sophie, the more he realized how much her opinion of him mattered. He remembered his first visit to her shop and how sure he was that she was scamming people. Once he met her in person, he didn't want to believe she had cheated his mother out of money. Instead, he kept hoping to be proved wrong about her.

Now that he thought about it, that was probably why he was so mad at himself that day. He didn't want to believe he could be fooled so easily by her. When his mother told him about Sophie knowing where to find his father's secret hiding place, he couldn't believe his ears. But the proof was right there before him, in the form of stock certificates. It was then he allowed himself to begin to believe in her gifts. He was drawn to her against his will; it was as if he couldn't help himself. This had never happened to him before with a woman. Usually, they enjoyed each other's company and sex until he grew tired of them. This woman was different; the more he thought about her, the more he wanted to spend time with her, and it didn't matter in what capacity.

He had even gone so far as to try to satisfy his need for her by taking Pamela to bed last night. If anything, it had made him realize that there was no emotion whatsoever to Pamela's lovemaking. He didn't think that she was capable of feeling any kind of deep emotional bond with anyone. He realized sitting across the table from Sophie this afternoon that he had more than just a passing interest in her. It suddenly dawned on him that she may already have a boyfriend. The thought had never occurred to him until just that moment, and it filled him with jealousy. This was a new feeling for him, and he didn't like it. He decided when he called his mother back that he would see what she knew about Sophie's personal life, if anything.

Finishing his dinner, he rinsed and recycled the cartons. Pushing the button on the answering machine, he listened to the messages. The first one was from his mother. "Hello, dear, it's Mom. I just wanted to remind you about dinner tomorrow night. Don't forget to bring Max with you. I have some goodies for you to take home for him. Oh, and don't forget to pick up the soft drinks. Love you, see you tomorrow night."

The second message was from Pamela. "I had a wonderful time last night at the opera and afterwards. I hear congratulations are in order. A little birdie told me about your Computek stocks. That's quite a windfall, now you'll be able to take your company to the next level. Now maybe you'll have a little more time to play. I have several more functions that I want to talk to you about going to. Give me a call when you get home."

Shaking his head, he wondered how Pamela had managed to find out about his mother's windfall. Supposedly only he, Matthew and the lawyer knew about the stocks.

Picking up the phone, he dialed his mother's number. She answered on the third ring. "Hey, Mom, how are you doing? I got your message. I won't forget the soft drinks, and yes, Max is coming along. Hey, I ran into your friend Sophie again last night at the opera. She was there with her aunt Antoinette."

"I hadn't realized that you'd met Sophie," she said, sounding curious. A suspicion was starting to form in her mind. "Nick, you didn't go down to Sophie's and give her a hard time, did you?" There was silence on the other end of the line. "You did, didn't you? I'm going to skin Matthew alive for telling you anything about my visits to Sophie."

"All right, I admit it, I went down there with the intention of accusing her of defrauding old women out of their money, but I never got the chance; instead, I ended up buying you something for your anniversary. I don't understand it, I had every intention of confronting her about it, but I never did. I was going to go back down there, but then I came to dinner and you told me about how she helped you find Dad's secret box. It was then that I realized she might be the real thing."

"Of course she's the real thing, silly boy. I have questions I ask that only your father would know. But with her, I didn't even get the chance to ask any questions. The first words out of her mouth were 'Did you find the secret panel yet?' Needless to say, I was blown away by that. When I told her I hadn't, she asked Bill where to find it. That's how I found your dad's secret hiding place."

"I'm sorry, Mom, I should never have interfered. I was only trying to protect you."

"Nick, I know you're trying to protect me, but your father's still with me, and he wouldn't let me make a fool of myself. Have you spoken to Sophie about this?"

"Um, I did go by Sophie's shop today, and we had lunch at the dog café. I did let her know the reason for my initial visit, and I apologized."

"Does she know that you're my son?"

"No, I didn't tell her that part."

"Nickolas Alexander Stavros, I'm surprised at you. You should've told her when you had lunch today. Well, she'll find out when she comes to dinner tomorrow night," she said, smiling to herself.

"You mean she's the guest that you invited to dinner? I was under the impression that it was someone your age," Nick said in surprise.

"I never said it was an older person; I just said I was inviting a friend to dinner and wanted you and Matthew to meet her. So you ran into Sophie and

Antoinette last night? They had invited me to go with them, but I had just too much to do yesterday."

"Well, I'll tell you something, Mom, if it hadn't been that the opera was supporting animal rescues, I wouldn't have gone either. But I'm glad I did, because the opera was really quite good."

"I'm glad you enjoyed it, dear. La Boheme was one of my and your dad's favorite operas. Why is it I get the feeling that there's something else you're not telling me?" Her comment was met with silence. "I knew it. What's going on?"

"Well, some strange things have been happening lately, and she's the only one I know who might have been able to help me."

"What sort of things?" she wanted to know.

He proceeded to tell his mother what he had told Sophie that afternoon. When he finished, he could hear her laughing. "What's so funny?"

"You are. It's about time you realized that just because you can't touch it, feel it, or see it, doesn't mean that it doesn't exist. You are so like your father. He was exactly the same way when we got married. That changed as the years passed. Your grandmother made no bones about her gifts, and your father learned over the years to trust her premonitions and feelings. I didn't know it at the time, but she was the one who advised him to buy the stock. I only found this out in a session with Sophie. You're just as stubborn as your father was."

"I hope that my having lunch with her won't upset her boyfriend. After all, it was a working lunch."

"Nickolas, if you want to know if she's married or has a significant other, why didn't you just ask me? The answer is no, she's not married, and she is not involved with anyone. She's not your usual sort, and I'm glad. It shows me that maybe you're finally looking for a meaningful relationship. If you want any type of relationship with Sophie, you have to accept her for who she is. She is a woman, but she is also a psychic medium, which is an integral part of her."

"Mom, I don't know if I'm ready for a permanent relationship."

"Honey, if you're interested in Sophie and not one of those other bimbos, then you're ready for a permanent relationship. The big question is if Sophie is interested in one with you. First thing you'll have to do is spend some time with her and find out what the life of a psychic medium is like."

"I really can't imagine what that's like. I guess I've got a lot to learn."

"Yes, you do. If your grandmother was alive, she could have helped you. Listen, dear, I've got to go. I'm baking my Athenian walnut cake for dessert for tomorrow night."

"Okay, Mom, I'll see you tomorrow," he said, hanging up the phone.

He would have to return Pamela's call and let her know that their relationship was over. It was not going to be a pleasant phone call, but a necessary one. He decided that he would call her after his workout. Heading for the bedroom, he changed into his workout clothes and returned to the kitchen to fill his water bottle. He was about to head downstairs to work out when the doorbell rang.

Wondering who was at the door, he decided to check the security monitor located on the kitchen wall to find out who it was.

"Crap, what the hell is she doing here?" he mumbled to himself, seeing Pamela standing at the front door. He pushed the intercom button on the monitor and told Pamela, "I'll be right there."

Max whined at him, and he reached down to rub his ears. "It's okay, boy, I don't think you need to be present for what's gonna happen next. Let's put you outside." Max, hearing the word "outside", headed for the back door. He let Max outside and headed for the front door. Opening the door, he let Pamela in and headed back into the kitchen, with her trailing behind him.

"So, what brings you here tonight? You look like you're headed to some function. I just got home an hour ago and was going to give you a ring."

"Well, darling, now there's no need for you to call me, because I'm here," she said, smiling up at him. "Aren't you going to take my coat?"

"No, Pamela, you're not going to be staying that long," he said with a frown on his face.

She took a quick look at his face and could tell by the tone of his voice and the set of his jaw that he was mad about something. "Why, whatever's wrong, darling?" she asked in a honeyed voice.

"You're what's wrong. Why did you tell Sophie that you're my fiancée? We are not nor have we ever been engaged. You knew at the outset that our relationship was one of mutual gratification, nothing more. I made no pretense that you were anything other than a bed partner and someone to accompany me to events, nothing more."

"I'm aware of how our relationship began, but after three years, I assumed it would become permanent. Neither one of us is getting any younger, you know. And besides, we're a perfect fit for each other in and out of bed. What does it matter if I told that woman we were getting married? She's nothing to either one of us, is she?" she asked, looking at him intently.

"My personal life is my own, and I will not allow anyone to dictate or force me into a relationship, not even you."

"Darling, far be it from me to try to force you to do anything you don't want to. I just thought as our relationship was growing that you'd want to make it permanent."

"This wouldn't happen to have anything to do with the stocks my father left for us, would it? By the way, how did you find out about those?"

"Darling, of course that hasn't got anything to do with that, you're being silly. As for me finding out about the stocks, my best friend is your mother's lawyer's secretary. It just kind of slipped out when we were talking the other day. What does it matter, Nick? We have so much in common. We complement each other very well in bed, we both have our own money and neither one of us wants to have children. We can do whatever we want, go wherever we want to go, without the complication of children getting in the way."

"Pamela, you have absolutely no idea of what I want or don't want. If you had ever bothered to ask me, I would have told you that I definitely want children. I enjoy working and seeing my company grow. I'm not the type of person to flit way my life going to parties and traveling. Obviously, we want different things out of life. I think it's time we put an end to our relationship."

"It's that bitch, isn't it? You've got the hots for her, don't you? I saw the way you looked at her the other night. I can tell you right now, she's not your type and never will be. I don't think she has the backbone or the passion to have a relationship with you. She's nobody, and she'll never be anything more than a two-bit pseudo psychic."

"And you, Pamela, have all the passion of a dead fish. I think you need to leave now," he said, opening the front door for her to leave.

"You'll regret this, Nicholas. I'll make sure that everyone knows how you treated me," she fairly screeched at him, pure venom in her look and voice.

"Pamela, how undignified of you. Be careful; you're beginning to sound like a common shrew. I'm not worried about it, people have been telling me for the last three years to get rid of you," he said, slamming the door behind her. *Wow, I feel like I've just done three rounds with Mike Tyson,* he thought to himself. He was glad that the whole thing was over and he didn't have to deal with her anymore. Heading for the back door, he let Max inside and set the alarm. Heading downstairs, Nick started his workout.

Back upstairs, Bert, Helen, Sid and Bill discussed what had just happened.

"Well, that wasn't so bad," Helen said. "I expected it to be worse than that."

"Me, too. She didn't put up much of a fight about the whole thing," Bill said.

"I'll tell you something, I've been through this before in several lifetimes. That was too easy, she's up to something. All we have to do now is wait for the other shoe to drop," Sid said.

"I'm afraid I'll have to agree with Sid. Remember the old saying, 'Hell hath no fury like a woman scorned.' I believe we haven't seen the last of her. As Sid said, it's just a matter of waiting to see what her next move will be."

Chapter 14

An hour later, her hair trimmed and styled, Sophie and JT were headed back to the shop when her cell phone rang. It was Toni calling.

"Hi, Toni, what's up?"

"I just finished getting everything set up for Dan's party. Come for dinner tonight so we can go over everything and make sure I didn't forget anything."

"All right, what time do you want me there?"

"How about five?"

"Five it is, I'll be there. I'm sure Teddy will be glad to have someone to terrorize besides you." Hanging up the phone, she arrived at her house.

She spent the next hour doing laundry, dishes and paying bills on her computer. Picking up her keys and purse, JT followed her out to the car. She headed the car towards Toni's house, turning on the radio and singing along all the way there. Arriving at the gates to her house, Sophie punched in the security number, and the gates opened to allow her up the driveway.

Getting out of the car, they headed for the side door leading to the kitchen. She found Tony inside putting the finishing touches on dinner. Teddy came running into the kitchen to greet JT, yapping excitedly.

"Something smells really good. Is that what I think it is, spaghetti with meatballs?"

"Of course, with fresh oven baked French bread."

"Will you stop that? I'm starting to drool."

"Well, grab the plates and silverware, and we'll eat here in the kitchen." Toni laughed.

Grabbing the hot pads, Toni placed them on the table and placed the spaghetti pot and French bread on the table. "I've got some fresh parmesan and a small salad for each of us in the refrigerator, if you want to get it out for us. Oh, there's also a couple of bones wrapped up in there for the guys."

Sophie dug in the refrigerator and found the salads, bones and parmesan. Unwrapping the bones, she gave one to each of the dogs. They both sat down, eating their dinner in silence, only commenting on how good the dinner was. Finishing their dinner, they gathered up the dishes, putting them in the sink and the leftovers in the refrigerator.

"Let's go into the living room. I've got all the information there."

Sophie kicked off her shoes and made herself comfortable in one of the big, overstuffed chairs. Toni picked up the folder on the table and handed it to Sophie, making herself comfortable in the other overstuffed chair.

"I decided to change up the theme a little bit for the party. I don't know if I told you, but Dan's been really getting into the whole paranormal thing over the last year or so. So I changed the party theme to all things paranormal, and since that's your field, I wanted to get your opinion."

"You're kidding, right? Dan is the last person I would have thought would be interested in the paranormal."

"If you think it's hard for you to believe, you should see it from my side. I'll tell you what started it all. Remember when he was gone last year in spring for two weeks? While he was staying at a hotel in San Francisco that was built in 1898, he was woken up in the middle of the night around 3 am to see this black, shadowy figure with red eyes leaning over him. He said it scared the living tar out of him, said it felt evil and menacing. He ended up staying up the rest of the night and checked out of the hotel the next morning. Ever since then, he's been doing a lot of research on this thing. He says he thinks it was a shadow person."

"It certainly sounds like it may be. These things are definitely negative, and not to be trifled with by someone who doesn't know what they're doing. I've had to deal with a lot of negatives, and it's never very pleasant."

"Let me show you the decorations that I have in mind." They spent the next hour and a half going over the decorations, food and party favors.

"What about the cake? I have a friend who could do a wonderful paranormal birthday cake. Let me order the cake, I have a brilliant idea that I think you'll both love."

"Great, I'll leave that to you, then. As long as it's not in the shape of a shadow person, he'll love it." They both laughed.

"Let's take the boys out for a walk around the property; that'll wear off some of our dinner," Sophie suggested.

"Oh, all right. I would rather turn into a couch potato, but you're right, we need to wear off some of our dinner." They spent the next hour exercising the dogs and themselves. Heading back inside the house, Toni prepared a couple of containers with leftovers in them for Sophie to take home with her.

"Now JT and I have dinner for most of next week. It will save me from having to cook," Sophie said, laughing. Her aunt helped her carry the containers of leftovers out to the car. Hugging her, she and JT climbed into the car and headed for home.

Arriving home, she gathered her containers and locked up the car, going inside. Once inside, she secured the door and went upstairs. Heading into the bedroom, she grabbed her nightgown and headed for the bathroom to take a shower. As she got ready for bed, her mind kept wandering back to her lunch with Nick that day. Slipping beneath the cool, soft sheets of the bed, she closed her eyes and was almost immediately asleep.

"Do you think we should tell her that Nick is Jewel's son?" Ann asked Martha.

"You'll learn over time that there are some things people need to find out for themselves. And at this point, it doesn't really matter, because she's going to find out tomorrow evening who he is anyway."

"Do you think she's going to be mad at us for not telling her?"

"She knows we can't tell her everything. She might be upset for a moment or two, but she'll get over it."

"She and Nick are going to end up together, aren't they? I'm able to see how they end up, but not the entire process."

"You'll find that the process is not as important as the outcome. As you gain more experience at this, you'll be able to see the entire journey from start to finish. Right now you're too impatient, so all you'll see is the beginning and the end. You need to slow down a bit and take it one step at a time," Martha told her.

"I'll try to slow down. I know I always seem to be in a hurry; it must be a holdover from my last life," she said, sighing.

"That could very well be. I need to check in with Michael right now, so I'm going to leave you here holding the fort," Martha said, disappearing.

Ann decided to settle down on the couch and wait for Martha to return. She couldn't have been sitting there for longer than a few minutes when she heard a soft whisper.

"Is she gone?"

She could tell by the accent that it was Sid. "Yes, Sid, she's gone."

"Well, it's about time, luv. I thought she was never going to leave. How are things going over here?"

"Not too bad, except for that Pamela woman. I really cannot stand her. The only thing good about her is she bought one of Bree's figurines."

"We thought he'd never get rid of her. He told her to shove off earlier today, but I've got a feeling we haven't seen or heard the last of her."

"Yeah, that is one vindictive woman, and I feel sorry for her guardians. She's so closed off, I don't know how anyone would ever get through to her."

"So how are we going to get these two together? Bert says they'll have to do it on their own and we're not supposed to interfere."

"Yes, Martha told me much the same thing. She says that there are some things that mortals have to figure out on their own, and it's not for us to interfere. I guess we just have to sit back and let nature take its course. But I'll tell you one thing, I'm not going to let Pamela interfere if I can help it."

"I'm with you there, luv, I'll do what I can on my end. I better get back, Bert will be missing me if I'm gone too long," he said, grinning.

"You mean he'll know you've been up to something if you don't," she said, laughing.

He grinned back and disappeared.

Sophie was up bright and early the next morning, dressed in shorts and an old T-shirt. After breakfast, she and JT went downstairs to the shop to begin her spring cleaning. She spent the entire morning cleaning the shop from top to bottom. Breaking for lunch, she and JT headed down the block to the Hungry Dog Café. After finishing their lunch, they took a leisurely walk around the neighborhood. By the time they arrived back at the shop, it was close to 90°, so she decided to vacuum and wash the car. Standing back from the car, she surveyed her hard work.

"There you go, big man; the car is clean and fresh, ready for our trip to see Jewel tonight." JT whimpered happily in response. "Let's go inside and take a rest and have a little ice cream."

JT headed for the door to the house and waited for Sophie to catch up. Emptying the bucket of dirty water, she washed out the rags and hung them on the fence to dry. Opening the door, they headed upstairs to the kitchen, where she scooped up some ice cream for herself and JT. She sat down on the couch and turned on the television to watch reruns of her favorite show, Paranormal State. An hour later, her shows were over.

"Don't you think it's time that you started getting ready to go to Jewel's?"

"I've got plenty of time. It's only 4 o'clock, and dinner's not until 6:30."

"What are you going to wear?" Ann asked.

"I'm not sure; just something simple and comfortable. Maybe the blue and gold sundress."

"I agree, the dress is beautiful and comfortable. You can wear the blue sandals with it," Ann said.

Pulling the dress out of the closet, she laid it on the bed, along with fresh underwear and her blue sandals. She rummaged in her jewelry box and pulled out a sterling silver embossed pit bull pendant necklace.

"Well, now that the hard part's done, I've got to go over the books for the week." Heading downstairs to the safe, she grabbed the ledger and headed back upstairs to the kitchen table. Turning on the computer, she opened her ledger and spent the next hour transferring the information to her computer. All the while she was working, JT slept under the table, snoring softly.

Pushing the enter button one more time, she could see by the balance that she had made $4000 this week.

"All right, JT, this was an extremely good week for us. I'll be able to put $1000 of the money into our savings account." Glancing at the clock, she suddenly realized that she only had 30 minutes to get ready before she needed to leave. Heading for the bathroom, she took a quick shower, applied her makeup and blow dried her hair. Twenty minutes later, she was stepping into fresh undergarments and slipping the sundress over her head. She put the necklace on and turned to look in the mirror. Looking over at JT where he lay at the foot of the bed. "Well, what do you think?" she asked him, twirling in front of him.

"I don't think he's easily impressed, but I think you look very nice," Martha said.

"I think you look lovely, the blue really sets off your eyes and hair," Ann said.

"Yeah, I do look pretty good, don't I?" she said, looking at her image again in the mirror. "All right, big man, are you ready to go?" she asked JT telepathically.

He bounded off the bed and headed towards the door. She grabbed her purse and keys and headed for the door. JT waited impatiently for her to catch up and open the door. Opening the door, JT bounded out towards the car, waiting impatiently at the gate for her to open it. Unlocking and opening the gate, JT headed for the driver's side back door of the SUV and sat down to wait for Sophie to open the door. She opened the door, and he jumped inside.

Plugging Jewel's address into the onboard GPS navigation system, she pulled out of the driveway. It took almost 30 minutes to arrive at Jewel's house. She noticed there were two other cars in the driveway, so she parked out front of the house. Climbing out of the car, she went around to the passenger side and let JT out. She headed towards the driveway and walked up to the front door, with JT close behind. Ringing the doorbell, Jewel soon answered the door.

"Sophie, so glad you could come. You brought JT with you; how lovely," Jewel greeted her.

"I brought you a bottle of Moscato; it's made from pears and apples," Sophie said, handing Jewel the bottle.

"Lovely, it sounds delicious," Jewel said, admiring the wine bottle. "Let's go into the living room. I want you to meet my sons." She noticed that only Matthew was in the living room. She wondered where Nick had gotten off to.

"Sophie, I'd like you to meet my youngest son, Matthew. Matthew, this is Sophie; she's the one who helped me find your father's papers."

Standing up, Matthew smiled and shook hands with Sophie. *Well, if I had known she was so gorgeous, I'd have gone to have a reading myself,* he thought. "It's very nice to meet you, Sophie, and who is this you have with you?" he asked. Reaching out, he rubbed JT's ears and told him, "You're certainly a big guy, aren't you? What breed is he?" he asked Sophie.

"He's a pit bull," she said, grinning at him.

"He's certainly the biggest one I've ever seen." Thinking to himself, *That's an understatement.*

"That's what I thought when I first saw him," Nick said, admiring Sophie's figure from behind.

Startled, Sophie's head swung around as she heard the familiar voice from behind her. Her expression mirrored the surprise she was feeling.

"Nick, I was wondering where you had gotten off to. I believe you've already met Sophie."

"Yes, Mother, I have." Looking directly at Sophie, he said apologetically, "If I had known that you were the guest Mother had invited for dinner tonight, I would have told you yesterday that she was my mother. I didn't find out until this morning that you were going to be here."

Sophie cocked her head to the side and was silent.

Nick watched her reaction closely and noticed a far-off look in her eyes, as if listening to a conversation that only she could hear. So, he waited for her attention to return to him.

"He's telling the truth, you know; he didn't find out until this morning," Bert said.

Turning her attention inward, she saw an older man and woman, along with a younger man, standing close by Nick. "And I take it you are his guides?" she asked the older man telepathically.

Martha spoke up. "Sophie, I'd like to introduce you to an old friend of mine, Bert. We've known each other for several millennia. The other two with him are Helen and Sid, they're guides in training."

"Nice to meet all of you. I see Bill has joined us for dinner tonight as well," Sophie said, nodding in the direction of the recliner where Bill was seated.

"Said he wouldn't have missed it for the world, luv," Sid said.

Bringing herself out of her reverie, she noticed that Nick was watching her intently. "That's all right. Obviously, I didn't put two and two together, and I didn't ask my guides about it either. They probably figured I'd know soon enough."

Nick noticed the exact moment when Sophie's attention returned to the room. He wished that he could hear and see what she heard and saw. "Where did you go just now?" he asked.

"Go?" she asked.

"When you zoned out there for a minute or two. Your eyes got a faraway look in them, like you were listening to a conversation somewhere else."

"Sorry, I didn't mean to be rude, but when my guides speak to me, I listen. This time, it was not only my guides, but yours also. Oh, and by the way, your father's here; he decided to join us for dinner. He told Sid he wouldn't miss it for the world."

"Who's Sid, dear?" Jewel asked, handing the bottle of wine to Matt.

"Nick has three guides. Bert, he's the head guide; he's been around for a long time. Then there's Helen and Sid, who are guides in training."

"I can feel them around me, and I get the impression that they're talking, but I can't hear what they're saying," Jewel said.

"So, Sophie, what are they saying?" Matt asked as he handed the wine bottle to Nick.

Sophie tuned in to Nick's guides. They told her about the first day when Nick came to her shop. How they prevented him from coming into the shop because he was so mad.

Listening to them, she started laughing. "What's so funny?" Matt wanted to know.

Still laughing, she said, "I don't think Nick's going to appreciate this one, but now it all makes sense to me." She went on to explain what happened to the others.

"The first day when Nick came to see me, he tried to open the door to the shop, but it wouldn't open. He thought the door was stuck. I thought it was odd, because I've never had that happen before or since. I've just been informed by his guides they knew he was angry and they wanted to give him time to cool off. So, they decided to keep the door from opening. They just told me that he thought I was a fraud," she said, looking over at him with a knowing look.

Nick was taken aback but tried not to show it. Suddenly, he heard his father's laughter, and he cautiously looked at his mom and brother to see if they had heard anything, but their expressions did not alter. Then he looked at Sophie and noticed a secretive smile on her face. He knew then that it was indeed his father he heard, and not a figment of his imagination.

Matt watched the exchange between the two of them with rapt attention. This was the first time he could ever remember his brother at a loss for words, and he was enjoying every minute of it.

"Nicholas Alexandros Stavros, tell me you didn't do that!" his mother said incredulously. Her voice was quiet and full of censure.

"Sophie, I would like to apologize for my behavior that day. I admit to being a narrow-minded non-believer at the time, but things have happened since then, and I've learned to be a little more open minded."

Matt nearly choked on his drink. "Now I've heard everything; this is a switch, Nick being open minded."

Nick scowled in his direction and started to say something when his mother cut him off.

"Matthew, stop baiting your brother and finish your drink. It's time for dinner. Nicholas, we'll talk later."

Nick knew his mother was upset with him and could fully understand why. He felt like a kid getting caught with his hand in a cookie jar.

Sophie couldn't help but smile at the dynamics of this family. Clearly, Jewel was the matriarch and ruled with an iron fist in a velvet glove.

"Nick, you and Matthew set the table, while Sophie and I will bring the dishes in the kitchen. Oh, and put the wine in the chiller for the dessert course," Jewel said and headed for the kitchen, with Sophie in tow.

"Hey, wait a minute, what about the dogs?" Matt wanted to know.

Sophie stopped, turned around and communicated telepathically with both dogs, telling them to follow Nick and Matt into the dining room and lay down.

The two men watched as both dogs got up and headed for Sophie, sitting down in front of her with their heads cocked and ears up, as if listening to something. Both dogs got up and sat next to Nick.

"I told them to go with you into the dining room, where they can lay down and wait for me." Turning, she followed Jewel into the kitchen.

"Mom told me she communicated telepathically with animals, but I didn't believe it. Wow, that's amazing. I wish I could learn to do that," Matt told his brother.

Once again, Nick had noticed a change in Sophie's demeanor as she communicated with the dogs. "Come on, let's get the table set. I've brought some soda, and we can put them in the wine chiller so they'll be ready for dinner."

They headed into the dining room, with the dogs following closely behind. Once there, the dogs headed to the corner of the room, where two large, overstuffed cushions lay on the floor. They made themselves comfortable and watched the two humans as they moved around the room.

In the kitchen, Jewel pulled the dishes out of the oven. "Sophie, you'll find a salad and some bottles of dressing in the refrigerator, go ahead and take them into the dining room. Oh, and can you take these hot pads and set them one on each end of the table for me? The door to my right will take you to the dining room."

Taking the salad out of the refrigerator, she headed into the dining room with it. Entering the dining room, she noticed that the table had been set and there were bottles of soda chilling in what she assumed was a wine chiller. The dogs were lying quietly on the cushions in the corner of the room. Setting the salad in the center of the table, she headed back into the kitchen and grabbed the hot pads and bottles of dressing out of the refrigerator and set them on the dining room table next to the salad. She entered the kitchen just as Jewel was taking a container of flatbread out of the oven.

"I can hardly wait to eat, everything smells so wonderful." Pointing to the dish Jewel just took out of the oven, she asked, "Those almost look like pita bread, but they're much too fluffy to be pita. What are they?"

"They are Armenian flatbread. I never got the knack for making them, so I buy them from a friend of mine who owns an Armenian bakery. Trouble is, I love the darn things, and they love me, too, in all the wrong places," she said, patting her hips.

"I'm with you there!" Sophie said, and they both laughed.

The kitchen door leading to the dining room opened up, and Matt stuck his head in the door. "Hey, what's going on in here? You've got two hungry guys out here waiting for food."

"All right, Matthew, we're coming. Do me a favor and grab a couple of serving utensils and the salt and pepper," Jewel said.

"Okay, Mom, will do."

Sophie and Jewel picked up the hot dishes and headed for the dining table. Arriving in the dining room, they found Nick placing glasses of ice next to each person's place setting.

"Nick, can you grab the bread out of the kitchen?" Jewel asked.

"Sure, Mom, be right back." As he was heading into the kitchen, Matt was coming out. Once in the kitchen, he grabbed a hot pad, tucked it under his arm, and grabbed a couple of potholders, taking the hot container into the dining room. "Matt, grab the hot pad under my arm and put it in the middle of the table for me, will you?" Matt did as he was asked and took his place at the table.

"What would you like to drink, Mom?" Nick asked. "I brought Pepsi, Coke, Sprite and flavored water."

"I'll have some of the flavored water, please." Nick handed her a bottle of the water.

"How about you, Sophie, what would you like?"

""I'll take the Sprite, thank you." Handing her the bottle, he took a seat next to his mother.

"So, Sophie, my mother said that you spoke to Dad and he told you where to find the hidden compartment. I find that absolutely amazing. Do you communicate telepathically?"

"Yes, it's kind of like picking up a telephone and getting an instant connection with the person. Sometimes they'll come to me for living people who have an appointment with me and give me information the person needs. Your father had been trying to get through to your mother for a long time but was getting nowhere. That's when he took matters into his own hands and got a hold of Jean. She, in turn, brought your mother to me."

"That's amazing, our grandmother and great-grandmother had abilities. Is there a way to increase a person's abilities?"

"Yes, absolutely. It's all about practicing and learning how to open yourself up to the other side."

Nick had been sitting quietly during the conversation, watching the exchange between Matt and Sophie. Matt appeared to be fascinated by Sophie, and they seemed to get along perfectly. The thought of his brother and Sophie together filled him with jealousy. It was an emotion he was not used to feeling, and in the short time he had known her, this was the second time he had experienced it.

"Sophie, do you know what the hidden papers contained?" Nick asked, drawing her attention back to him.

"No, whenever a spirit gives me information about a package or object, I don't want to know anything about it. I don't believe that it's any of my business. If the spirit wanted me to know what was in it, they would have told me."

"Mom, do you want to tell Sophie what was in the hiding place?" Nick asked her.

"That's one of the reasons I invited you here tonight, Sophie. I wanted to let you know how important the papers we found are to my family. The papers contained within the hidden lockbox were shares in Computek Corporation from when it was first conceived. My husband bought them when they first formed Computek and were looking for investors. Every now and then, he would get a wild notion to do something and then just do it, I wouldn't find out for, sometimes, years later. About half of the things either bought or invested in turned out to be viable in some small way. This time he made a really good decision, and made it even better by holding on to the shares. We found the shares are worth over two million dollars."

"Well, it sounds like he really did make a good decision this time. I'm so glad you were able to find the papers."

Setting her napkin down on the table, Jewel got up from the table and walked over to the breakfront on the far side of the dining room, opened a drawer and pulled out an envelope. Coming back to the table, she handed Sophie the envelope and sat back down. "I wanted you to benefit from our good fortune, because if it wasn't for you, we would still be looking for and not finding it. Please, open the envelope."

Nick was not surprised by his mother's actions; he knew she felt she would never have found the papers if it wasn't for her. He had to agree, he was sure they would never have found the papers any time soon.

Opening the envelope, Sophie withdrew a cashier's check made out to her in the amount of fifty thousand dollars. She was sure that the shock was reflected on her face. The next thought that crossed her mind was that Nick would be proven right about her being after his mother's money. Looking over at Nick, she expected to see a look of accusation on his face, but instead she saw that he was smiling.

Nick watched the play of emotions reflected on her face and could tell that she was shocked by the amount of the check. His mother had come to him with the idea of giving Sophie a finder's fee for her part in finding the papers. He thought it was a great idea and told his mother so. She had kept some of the money for herself. He left it to his mother's discretion on what she gave Sophie.

"Jewel, I just can't accept this money, it's way too much," she said, looking at Jewel.

"Honey, you can do whatever you want with the money. Don't you have a favorite rescue or two that could use some money? Keep some for yourself, but you can also donate some to the rescues," Jewel suggested.

"What a wonderful idea; I think I'll do just that. Thank you so much. I know the rescues will be grateful for the donations," she said with tears in her eyes.

"That's it, then. Now that we've got that all settled, let's have dessert," Matthew said cheerfully.

"I bought a New York style cheesecake and some toppings, perfect for dessert," Jewel said. Getting up from the table, she started for the kitchen and turned to look at Matt. "Can you give me a hand, Matt?"

Matt noticed that his mother was looking at him meaningfully. Glancing at his brother and Sophie, he grinned to himself and headed for the kitchen.

"Sophie, I really want you to have this money. I know you're very active in several different rescues, and this money will help you help them. My mother sold the stocks and invested half of it back into our business. This will allow us to be able to expand and hire more employees. I told my mother you would probably give most of it away to the animal rescues, but she insists half of it be used for yourself, because you never know when an emergency is going to come up," Nick told her.

"Thank you. You know, I didn't expect you to agree with your mother's decision regarding the money. Not after the way that you felt when you first came to my shop."

"Will I ever be able to live that one down?" he asked her, grinning wryly. "I wanted to ask you a question."

"All right, ask away."

"I'd love to have lunch with you sometime this week, but I have a busy week. I want you to know that I'm going to call you every night."

Cocking her head to one side, she asked, "So exactly what is your relationship with Pamela at this time?"

"I want to be upfront with you about this. We had a mutually beneficial relationship for the last three years. I let her know in the beginning that there was never a chance for it to turn into anything permanent, but obviously she had other thoughts that I wasn't aware of," Nick told her.

"I want to be equally honest with you, I'm not looking for a short-term relationship. And I could never be in a relationship with anyone who did not understand or respect what I do and who I am."

"For years, I didn't believe that I'd ever want any kind of a permanent relationship, but since I met you, my opinion on that has changed. You've helped me open my mind to experiences and things that I had never thought about before. You and my father have both helped me see that there is life after death. I want you to help me to learn more about you and your gifts. That is, if you're interested."

She didn't answer for several moments, and once again her eyes took on a faraway look.

"Come on, Sophie, what are you waiting for?" Ann asked.

"Sophie, look within yourself and examine your feelings for him. Do you love him?" Martha asked.

"Yes, but I don't know if what he feels for me is love or a passing fascination."

"I can tell you this," Bert said, "he has never felt so strongly about a woman before. And I can tell you that he is experiencing jealousy when he thinks of you even talking to another man. That in itself has to tell you something about how he feels."

"All right, I'll do it. I'll take a chance on him!" Sophie told them.

Nick waited for her inner conversation to finish, and she returned to the present. He wished he could have been privy to the conversation that had just occurred in her mind. He waited patiently for her to respond to his last question.

"All right, I'm willing to give it a try. You're already more open than you were when I first met you. And both our guides think it's a good thing that everything will work itself out. They've never been wrong before, and I trust her judgment."

"I take it you were talking to them a few seconds ago?"

"Yes, how did you know?"

"As I said earlier, you get an unfocused, faraway look in your eyes when you're communicating with them. Like you're physically here, but checked out mentally."

"Yes, I've been told that before, although most people don't usually notice."

Meanwhile in the kitchen, Matt and Jewel had an ear glued to the door, listening to see how things were going. "It sounds like things are going well. I'll tell you one thing, Mom, if Nick wasn't going to go out with her, I certainly would have. I think she'll be exceptionally good for Nick."

"This is what I've been hoping for, I think they'll be perfect together. And maybe I'll get some grandchildren out of it, as you don't seem to be inclined in that direction either," Jewel said, pulling the toppings out of the refrigerator and setting them on a tray, along with some spoons. "You grab the tray, and I'll bring in the cheesecake."

Pushing the door open, Jewel entered the dining room, cheesecake in hand. "I hope you like cheesecake, Sophie. I have several different toppings that you can put on them if you'd like. Both of these boys love cheesecake, and it's one of the few desserts that I make well."

Everyone sat down while Nick opened the wine Sophie had brought and ate their dessert. Finishing their dessert, Nick suggested that they all go into the back yard and enjoy the waning evening sun.

Grabbing their drinks, everyone headed to the back yard, the dogs following behind. A large wicker table and chairs sat on a brick patio. There were several citronella candles placed around the area to prevent mosquitoes.

"What a wonderful space to have for an evening meal or just to sit here and enjoy the weather," Sophie said, admiring the lush green grass and the flowers surrounding the perimeter of the back yard. She noticed that JT and Max were having a great time running around the backyard, playing together.

They spent the next couple hours discussing everything from dogs to the best places to eat in town. The sun was beginning to set when Sophie noticed it was almost 9:30.

"I want to thank you for a wonderful dinner and great company," Sophie told Jewel. "I hate to break up the party, but I have to be up early tomorrow morning to do some yard work before it gets hot. It's the only quiet time I have to get the yard work done."

"We've all had such a wonderful time, and I'm glad you enjoyed the dinner. We need to do this again soon."

"I would like that very much." Impulsively, she asked Jewel, "I know that you and my aunt Toni have become good friends. We're having a surprise birthday party for her husband next weekend, and I'd like to invite you all to come."

"I'd love to come. I've met Dan a couple of times and think he's a great guy." Looking at Matthew and Nick, she asked, "What about you two? You don't have any pressing engagements next weekend, do you?"

"We'll both be there. Just send Mom all the information, and I'll make sure that we're there on time," Nick told her.

"I feel that I should let you know that there's a theme to the birthday party. And here's the kicker, it is a ghost or paranormal themed birthday party. Over the last year and a half, Dan has been really into the paranormal; he's even joined an investigative team and enjoys investigating in what little spare time he has."

"What does that mean exactly? Do we have to dress up like a ghost or something, or are the gifts supposed to be paranormal themed?" Matt asked.

"Either one. Some people find it fun to dress up in costumes, but it's entirely up to you. I'm actually going as a gypsy with a crystal ball," Sophie said, laughing.

They all laughed at the thought of her dressed like a gypsy and holding a crystal ball.

"I'd better get going, then." Calling out telepathically to JT, he trotted over to her side and sat down.

"Let me walk you out to your car," Nick said. Standing up, he guided her into the house, where she picked up her purse and keys. Nick followed her out the front door to where her SUV was parked out front. Nick opened the back passenger side door, and

JT jumped into the seat. Nick walked around to the driver side front door and opened it. Sophie turned to face him, and he reached out and pulled her into his arms.

The kiss seemed to go on forever, and when he finally let her go, he had to take a deep breath to calm himself. All he wanted to do was pick her up, take her to his home and make love to her all night. But he knew it was too early in their relationship to do that.

Sophie tried to catch her breath as he released his hold on her. The feeling she got from the kiss was the most amazing thing she had ever experienced. It felt passionate, sensitive, loving and protective all at once. The embrace left her feeling alone and bereft, as if she were only truly whole when she was in his arms.

Nick pulled his cell phone out of his pocket. "I don't have your home phone or your cell phone number. Can you give it to me?"

She gave him both numbers, as well as the shop number, and he in return gave her his home number, cell and work number.

"I've got a full week with several new projects starting this week, but I'm going to call you to set up a lunch date."

"Okay, if you can't reach me, leave a message and I'll call you back. I'm fully booked with readings myself."

Sophie made the drive home in a haze. Once she arrived home, she got ready for bed and didn't even bother to check her answering machine or emails. Falling into bed, she dreamt of them together in bed.

Nick, on the other hand, was full of pent up sexual frustration; to combat it, he spent the next hour in his gym working out.

"I think that went well, don't you?" Bert asked Martha.

"Yes, indeed, extremely well. Now we just have to keep the momentum going."

"I really don't think that's going to be a problem, luv," Sid said. "He's thinking about how he can help her by renovating her storefront for her right now."

"You're kidding, right?" Ann asked.

"No, actually I'm not. He's drawing up the plans in his mind right now."

"Wow, I hope he's going to expand it, her shop is too small, and she needs more room," Ann told him.

"Yup, and then some," Sid said, grinning.

Chapter 15

The following week flew by for Sophie, filled with readings and trips to the local rescue centers to help with traumatized animals. Even though she was busy most of the week, she still couldn't shake the feeling of increasing anxiety as the week wore on. She felt like she was waiting for something bad to happen. She didn't get the feeling very often, but when she did it usually heralded something negative was about to happen.

True to his word, Nick called her every evening, and they spoke for at least an hour each night. They talked about anything and everything except for how much they needed each other. She could hear it in his voice whenever he said goodnight to her.

Nick was having an exhausting and hectic week. Two new projects were set to begin, and he was spending a lot of time in the office, weeding through applications for new hires. He'd rather be working on a job site instead of stuck in the office doing interviews.

He had gotten two phone calls this week from new clients to cancel their renovation projects. The odd thing is that both of these clients were ones that he had gotten through referrals from Pamela. Fortunately, they were both small projects. He had also gotten calls from a couple of his friends, who told him that Pamela had been spreading rumors about his company being financially unstable. He remembered her saying that he would be sorry, and he figured this is her way of payback.

He had a follow-up appointment with Henry and Catherine tomorrow to go over information on both of their projects. He knew that Sophie was having a similar type of week. He hoped that Pamela wouldn't try to cause problems for her. The phone on his desk rang.

"Nick, someone named Sophie is on the line for you. Do you want me to take a message, or will you take the phone call?" Adele asked.

"No, I'll take it. Which line is she on?"

"She's on line 2."

"Oh, and Adele, whenever Sophie calls, make sure that you put her through to me, or at least call me and let me know she's on the line."

"Sure, Nick, no problem," she said, hanging up.

Wow, now there is a first, she thought to herself, *he had never taken a direct phone call from any of his women before.* She had been working for him for 10 years, and she had always taken messages from all of his current women. "Finally," she grumbled to herself, "it's about time he found a real woman, and not a disposable one."

He was surprised; this was the first time Sophie called him at work, so it must be something important.

"Hey there, this is the first time you've called me at work. I take it its something important, otherwise you wouldn't call me at work."

"I know you're going to think I'm crazy, but all week I've been having this awful feeling, like something bad is either going to happen or is happening."

"No, I don't think you're crazy; it's definitely been one of those weeks. I lost two clients, fortunately they were small renovations. But it still bothers me to lose them."

"I'm sorry to hear that, I kind of figured that something was up, but I don't think it's over yet. I get the feeling that someone is trying to cause problems."

"Yes, you could say that. Someone is definitely trying to make problems for me, but it's nothing I can't handle."

"Well, if everything is okay, I'll talk to you tonight. I have a client due any moment now."

"Hey, not so fast. I was going to call you anyway and ask if you'd like to go to the Animal Expo this weekend? They'll have a lot of rescues represented there, and I like to go every year. It starts on Saturday at 10 o'clock. I know we have the party on Saturday, but we could go Sunday and take the dogs with us. How about I pick up you and JT around 10:30, and we'll head over there?"

"That sounds wonderful. I think the boys will enjoy it. I've gotta go. I'll see you tomorrow," Sophie said, hanging up the phone.

Nick was smiling as he hung up the phone in anticipation of their weekend together. Finishing the paperwork on his desk, he grabbed his laptop and headed out of his office.

"Adele, I'm heading out to the Stevens and Palos sites. You can get me on the cell."

"Are you coming back to the office afterwards?"

"No, I'm gonna make it an early day. I've been invited to a birthday party, and it has a theme to it," he told her, grinning.

"What kind of a theme is it?"

"You're gonna laugh, but the theme is paranormal, you know, ghosts and things."

"I didn't think you believed in that sort of thing."

"I didn't, but there's been so many things happening lately to me and around me that it's opened up a whole new world for me."

"That means you've had a recent paranormal experience, probably at your house," she guessed, grinning at him.

"What makes you think I've had a paranormal experience recently?"

"Because people I know who have been skeptics, once they have their own experience, it turns them into a believer real quick. I've had my own encounters, so I'm definitely a believer."

"Listen, I gotta get going," Nick said, heading out the door. "If my brother calls, tell him to call me on my cell."

Sophie hung up the phone after talking with Nick and wondered what he wasn't telling her. She had no right to probe further into the situation, but she sure wished she could help in some way. The bell over the shop door rang, and she knew her client had arrived and it was time to go back to work.

The rest of the day passed in a blur of activity, and before she knew it, it was time for dinner. Changing into her pajamas, she sat down and made a phone call to her aunt. The phone rang several times before Antoinette answered.

"Hello there, Auntie, I take it Dan made it home on time."

"Actually, he got home earlier than I thought. It's a good thing I had everything put away for the party."

"How are you going to get him out of the house tomorrow?"

"Oh, I've got that all covered. He's thinks that Catherine is having a fundraiser for animals, and he has a weak spot for anything dog related. I told him I was helping her with preparations and he has to be here at 3:30."

"My, you're devious, aren't you? I just wanted to give you a heads up that I invited four more people to the party."

"Really? I hope at least one of them is a male younger than eighty," she said, half-seriously.

"Actually, I do have some news for you. You remember Nick? You met at the opera."

"The good looking guy who was there with Catherine's niece?"

"Yeah, that's the one. We're dating now, and it seems to be going pretty good."

"Is he aware that you're not into short-term relationships? I got the impression from him that he was a no-nonsense type of guy. Correct me if I'm wrong, but I would peg him as an 'I would have to see it to believe it' type of guy."

"He's well aware of my thoughts on short-term relationships. When I first met him, he was an absolute skeptic. But he's had his own paranormal experiences recently, and it's really opened his eyes."

"That's wonderful, it's about time you found somebody who really cares about you."

"His younger brother, mother and Brittany are coming, too. I think Nick's younger brother Matthew and Brittany will make a good pair."

"Ah, there's a method to your madness. Well, I'll do my best to help the situation along. Do you still plan on doing readings for the party? Don't forget to bring your crystal ball with you," she said, laughing.

"Yes, I still plan on doing 10-minute readings for the party. I thought I would dress like a gypsy and use a crystal ball as a prop. It will add some fun and flare to the party."

"I love the idea. It should be hilarious to see how people react. I'm so wound up and excited about the party, I'm not sure I'll be able to sleep tonight. I'd better calm down, otherwise Dan will know something's up, and I want this to be a complete surprise. I invited Catherine, Henry and his wife and Jane to come."

"Sounds like we're going to have a great party. Is there anything else you need me to bring?"

"No, I've set up a place for anyone who wants to bring their dogs and hired someone to take care of them."

"What a great idea. I'm sure JT will be excited to make some new friends. What time do you want me there tomorrow?"

"The party is at 3, and the caterers will have finished by 2:00, so how about 2:15? That way, you can help me finish up a few things."

"All right, I'll be there. Now get some sleep."

Hanging up the phone, she was excited at the thought of seeing Nick again. She fell asleep thinking of being in his arms again.

"Martha, we need to talk," Bert said telepathically.

"Ann, Bert needs to talk to me. I'll be right back."

"Sure, I'll keep watch, let me know what's up," Ann said, knowing that if Bert needed to speak with Martha alone, it must be something important.

Martha thought of Bert and was instantly next to him.

"I wanted to let you know Sid was talking with Pamela's guardians. He asked them what she was up to, because he didn't like the feeling he was getting from her. They were quite closed-mouthed, and that's never a good sign. She knows that Nick is very interested in Sophie, and she thinks he dumped her because of it. She definitely had other plans for Nick, so now she's out for blood," Bert told Martha.

"I agree, it's not a good sign when they're not forthcoming. It makes me think she's up to something. I wish I could make them tell me, but I can't, so I'll have to keep my eyes open."

"I just wish I knew what she was up to besides trying to make things difficult for Nick. Humans tend to create more problems than they solve."

"Well, I'll keep my eyes open and let you know if anything comes up."

"And I'll do the same," Bert told her. Giving her a hug, he disappeared from view.

Martha arrived back from her talk with Bert, deep in thought.

"So what did Bert have to say?" Ann asked anxiously.

"He wanted to let me know that he thinks Pamela's up to something, and it might include Sophie."

"Great, I don't like not knowing what that woman is up to; I don't trust her," Ann said.

"I don't either, so we had better keep our eyes open," Martha said, settling down on the couch to wait for morning.

Chapter 16

The morning of the party dawned bright and clear. Doing her morning accounts and housekeeping, she managed to get JT into the bathtub for a bath.

"Come on, old man, it's time for your bath. I have to make you smell good for the party tonight," she told him.

"There's nothing wrong with the way I smell, and you know I don't like baths," he complained telepathically.

"If you want to go to the party with me tonight and visit with Teddy, Max and Zeus, we need to make sure you're clean. There will also be some new dogs you've never met before, so you have to look and smell your best."

"Oh, all right." Climbing into the bathtub, he stood still while she washed and rinsed him. Climbing out of the bathtub, he started to shake himself off but heard her say, 'No shaking.' She toweled him dry and let him outside to shake the excess water off.

The morning passed in a whirlwind of activity around the shop. It was early afternoon when she picked up the phone to call Bree.

The phone rang several times before Bree picked up the line.

"Hello?"

"Hi, it's me." Before she could get another word out, Bree cut her off, sounding frazzled.

"Oh, thank God it's you! I am in desperate need of a spooky outfit to wear. I can't seem to think of anything to wear."

"Not to worry, I thought this might be an issue for you, so I picked up a spooky Victorian ghost costume. I'll come over around one, and that will give me time to help you get ready."

"Perfect, thanks so much, Sophie," Bree said. Letting out a sigh of relief, she hung up the phone.

A couple of hours later, Sophie loaded up her costume, a small folding table, tablecloth and crystal ball into the car. JT got into the back seat and whined softly, excited to see his new friend Zeus.

Arriving at Brittany's house, she let JT out, grabbed the costumes and headed inside. They spent the next forty-five minutes getting ready for the party. She had found a flowing tattered gossamer white gown for Bree that looked both ghostly and alluring at the same time.

She had created her own colorful gypsy costume out of fabric she had found online. The skirt was in multiple hues of blues, and it was long and flowing with a handkerchief hem that fluttered when she moved. The top was a white low cut peasant blouse tucked into the skirt. Big hoop earrings and multiple bracelets adorned both wrists, and a blue handkerchief was tied over her flowing hair.

"What did you get for Dan's present?" Bree asked.

"Do you remember that ghostly vortex sculpture you did? I decided to keep it and give it to Dan for his birthday," she said, grinning.

"Perfect, I'm glad you decided to keep it instead of giving it to your friend. I'll make another one for him. I had a dream a few weeks ago and was inspired to create a sculpture from the dream. It's a stairway to the clouds, and it turned out wonderfully. I think he'll like it."

"I'm sure he will love it." Looking at her watch, Sophie was surprised to find out they only had thirty minutes to make it to the inn. "Wow, where has the time gone? We need to leave now if I'm going to be there early to help Toni with the finishing touches."

Leaving the house, everyone piled into the SUV and they were on their way. Arriving at the Stone Cliff Inn, they were greeted by Toni. "See that large canopied area over there?" she said, pointing to an area to the right of where the outside party area was located. "That's where the dogs are going to be. Sophie, you remember Jill Harper? She's going to be taking care of the dogs."

"Yes, I remember her. She's got some intuitive abilities that work well with animals. I can see that Teddy's already anxiously awaiting JT's arrival and he's curious about Zeus."

"Go ahead and drop off the dogs, and we'll set your table up. That's all there is left to do."

Leading Bree over to the pet area, she spoke with Jill for a few minutes, then they headed over to the large patio area. The central patio had two smaller decks attached to it on both sides.

"You can set up your table on the back patio so that you have a bit of privacy," Toni said, pointing to a small deck in the opposite side of the central patio where a small tent was set up. "I'm going to have you doing the readings before and after the cutting of the cake and gift opening. That way, you have a chance to eat and mingle. We'll open the presents right after the cake cutting."

"That sounds good to me, and 10-minute readings will give everyone a chance to get one."

As she was talking, she sensed Toni's attention being drawn elsewhere. Before she could even turn her head, she felt Nick's vibrant presence. Turning her head, she saw Nick, Jewel, Matthew and Max entering the walkway.

"Looks like Nick and his family have just arrived," Toni said.

"Yes, let's go over, and I'll introduce you." Taking Brittany's arm, she led them both to meet Nick's family.

Nick's eyes were immediately drawn to where Sophie was standing with her aunt and friend. She was wearing a colorful gypsy-like costume which hugged her figure beautifully. She was heading toward where they were standing.

Stopping in front of them, Sophie introduced everyone. "Toni, I know you've already met Nick. The young man next to him is his younger brother, Matt, and this lovely lady is his mother, Jewel. Jewel, Matt, I'd like you to meet my aunt Antoinette and my best friend Brittany."

"Pleasure to meet you both. Catherine has spoken of you often, Antoinette. Bree, how nice to finally meet the genius behind the sculptures in Sophie's shop," Jewel said, shaking both of their hands.

"Just call me Toni; I don't stand on formality," she said, shaking their hands. "I didn't know Nick had a brother, very nice to meet you." Turning to Nick, she told him, "You can take Max over to the pet area and drop him off, Sophie will show you where and introduce you to the caregiver.

Matt, why don't you take Bree inside to get something to drink while I talk to your mom?"

"It would be my absolute pleasure," Matt said, grinning at Bree. Taking her by the arm, he led her inside the log cabin-like structure.

Bree was a little nervous, and she could sense an uncertainty in him, which instantly calmed her nerves. "You're not like your brother; you're more open to the other side, like your mother."

"Yeah, you could say I'm the polar opposite. He has all the drive and intensity, and I'm more laid back and easygoing," he said, laughing.

"That may be true in a sense, but you have just as much drive as he does, it just doesn't show itself in the same way. You like to paint for relaxation; it takes you into a whole other world and state of mind," she said, surprising herself on how easily his energy came to her. She had never had someone who she was so instantly connected to.

He looked at her in surprise, taken aback at her accuracy and the sense of rightness he felt being with her. "You're dead on, are you a psychic medium like Sophie?"

"I do have abilities, but nowhere near as good as hers are. This is the first time I've felt such a strong connection to anyone before. I feel like I've known you for a long time."

"That's funny, I was just thinking the same thing myself. Let's get a drink and go sit down and talk." A thought just occurred to him. "I'm sorry, I should have asked if you were here with someone," he said, wondering if she had a boyfriend who just hadn't arrived yet.

She smiled at him and decided to tease him a little. "Yes, I came with Zeus, Max and Sophie."

Matt felt a sharp stab of jealousy, looking around for the guy who came with her and decided he must be out on the patio. "Oh, sorry, I don't want to step on anyone's toes. I don't see anyone but the staff in here," he said, handing her a cup of sparkling apple cider.

"They're outside. I'd like to introduce you," she said, retracing her steps back outside. Pausing for a moment, she got her bearings and headed for the pet area, with Matt in tow.

He couldn't understand why he was jealous; he had only just met her. All he knew was that he wanted to get rid of the other guy and take his place in her life. She stopped for a moment, as if she were looking for someone, then she was leading him over to the pet area. He didn't see anyone but the caregiver. She stopped at the gate, and a good-sized pit bull came to the gate.

"Matthew, I would like you to meet Zeus. Zeus, this is Matt, can you say hi?"

Matt let out a sigh of relief that Zeus was a dog and not a man, although that still did not tell him if she had one in her life. He hadn't noticed any rings on her left hand, so he knew she wasn't married, but that didn't mean she wasn't seeing someone.

The dog sat down and lifted its paw to shake. Matt solemnly shook Zeus's paw. "Nice to meet you, Zeus." The dog wagged its stub and moved closer to Bree.

"Zeus is my seeing eye dog, roommate and the love of my life," she told him earnestly.

He felt an overwhelming sense of relief knowing that there was not another man in her life. His relief was quickly followed by a sense of surprise at finding out she was blind. It never even occurred to him that she might be blind; she moved without hesitation or awkwardness. "I would have never guessed you were blind, you move with such confidence. It's wonderful to see someone who is so confident in their abilities."

Bree felt a rush of joy at his words, and her connection with him seemed to grow stronger with his words. "There's a trick to it. If you count your steps and note the things you hear around you, you'll keep your sense of direction and won't get lost. I just got Zeus a couple of weeks ago, and we are still learning each other," she said, smiling. Stepping away from the gate, she turned towards the patio. "Maybe we can find a couple of seats on the patio and finish our drinks."

Matt could see that Nick was busy helping Sophie set up something and his mother was busy talking with Toni. "Sure, let's find somewhere comfortable to sit," he said, leading her back towards the patio.

"I'm going to be doing 10-minute readings for the party," Sophie informed Nick. "Can you help me get the table and things out of the car?" she asked him.

"Sure, no problem. Where are you going to set up?"

"Over there," she said, pointing to the small deck on the far side of the main patio.

"All right, go and back your vehicle at the entrance, and I'll help you unload it."

Sophie headed to the car and backed it up in front of the entryway. Nick made short work of unloading her items, and Sophie moved the car back into a parking space. Heading back to the small deck, she could see that Nick was already setting up the table and chairs inside the tent. Once the table was set up, Sophie unpacked the box containing the other props. Draping a silver cloth over the table, she arranged a large crystal ball in the center, with smaller crystals surrounding it. Small glass jars filled with sage and black salt were used for decoration. Standing back, she surveyed her handiwork. It definitely looked like a fortune teller's table. She placed her business cards on the table and fanned them out.

"It looks great, fit for a gypsy," Nick said from behind her, grinning at her.

She stuck her tongue out at him and laughed. She reached up, kissed him, and Nick pulled her close to him, relishing in her response to his embrace.

When Nick released her, it took her a moment to catch her breath. Nick was shocked at the intensity of his response to her. His body had grown rock hard just holding her.

Looking towards the cabin, he noticed Toni and Jewel were just coming out of the building. Matt and Bree were coming out of the garden area holding hands.

"Nick, there you are. I'm glad to see you helped Sophie get her tent set up. The tent looks wonderful, and I'm sure you're going to be very busy today," Jewel said.

"You've done a wonderful job as usual, Sophie. Jewel and I were wondering if you and Nick would help us put the rest of the spooky decorations."

"Of course we will. Come on, Nick, you can help me scatter the ghosts, cobwebs and ghouls around the patio and smaller decks." She smiled at him and took him by the hand. "Bree, can you and Matt keep an eye on my tent?"

"All right, I need to soak up the atmosphere here anyway. I think I have a couple of ideas for new sculptures. Oh, and by the way, I found out that they filmed parts of that Twilight movie here. Isn't that wonderful? I loved that movie." She sighed.

Sophie saw Matt roll his eyes when she mentioned the name of the film. Grinning, she winked at him, and he smiled.

Heading inside with Toni and Jewel, they grabbed several ghostly props and headed back outside and started setting them up. There were statues of headstones, ghosts, ghouls. They finished arranging the statues, then went back inside to grab the rest of the decorations. Another 10 minutes, and they were ready to receive guests. Dan arrived just as they finished spreading the cobwebs across the entryway.

"Dan, great to see you, how was your trip?" Sophie asked.

"Hey Sophie, didn't know you were coming to Catherine's party. The trip was exhausting, but I got three new clients out of the trip."

"Dan, I would like you to meet Nick Stavros. He owns Stavros Construction."

"Good to meet you, Nick, your dad and mine were friends for many years. They used to play poker together once a month on Sunday afternoon. I'm sorry for your loss."

"Thank you," Nick said, shaking his hand.

"Where's that wife of mine hiding?" he asked Sophie.

"She's inside talking to Jewel, Nick's mom."

"Great, I heard Teddy barking and went by to say hello."

They arrived inside to see Toni with a big grin on her face and holding a big sign which said, 'Happy Birthday to the man I love.'

Dan stopped dead in his tracks, then hurried over to where his wife stood holding the sign. Pulling the sign out of her hands and handing it to Jewel, who was standing beside her, he pulled her into his arms and kissed her.

When Dan released her from his embrace, she whispered to him, "If this is how you respond when I hold the sign, I'm going to hold one every day when you come home from work."

He grinned down at her and said, "You do that, and we'll never get out of bed."

"Hey, you two, get a room, will ya?" Nick said, grinning.

"We would, but we have a birthday party to attend," Toni said, grinning.

Looking around, Dan noticed all of the ghostly decorations. It was then that he noticed his wife was dressed like a mid-century ghoul and Sophie was dressed like a gypsy.

"What a great theme for a party. You've outdone yourself, my love, and those ghosts are great," he said, grinning like a little boy in a room full of toys.

"I knew you'd like it. Darling, it looks like our guests are starting to arrive, we'd better go to the door and greet them," she said, taking his hand.

"I'm going to head to the tent so that Bree can introduce your brother to Dan," Sophie told Nick.

He gave her a quick kiss and told her, "I'll get us something to drink, any requests?"

"How about a Shirley Temple with extra grenadine?" she said, wiggling her eyebrows at him.

He laughed and pulled her into his arms for a deep kiss. Releasing her, he headed for the bar that was set up at the far end of the room.

She headed for the tent, only to find Bree and Matt deep in conversation. They seemed to be engrossed in each other, to the exclusion of everyone and everything else. She smiled to herself, glad to see that her plan to get Matt and Bree together was working.

"Hey, you two, thanks so much for watching the tent for me. Bree, why don't you take Matt to meet Dan? I think the two of them have a lot in common."

"What do you mean? What do they have in common?" Bree asked.

"They're both believers and are fascinated by spirits. Matt, why don't you talk to Dan about going along on an investigation with his paranormal group?" Sophie suggested.

"I love it. Matt, I think you should go, and I'm going to talk to Dan about taking you," Bree told him. Taking his hand, she led him in search of Dan.

As he was coming out of the building carrying the drinks, Nick noticed Matt and Brittany heading inside, hands entwined. He had a fleeting thought that maybe, just maybe Sophie was trying to play matchmaker.

"Hey, I just saw Matt and Brittany heading inside, and it's a funny thing, they were holding hands."

"Really? Now who would have thought?" Sophie said, grinning.

"You wouldn't be playing matchmaker, would you?"

"Not really, but can I help it if I introduce two people and there is a mutual attraction?"

"Of course not. By the way, it seems rather odd to me that a blind woman was leading my brother by the hand. Should that be the other way around?"

"Not really. Whenever Brittany goes somewhere new, she counts the steps from one point to another so that she can find her way around. She's taking Matt to meet Dan; she's going to talk to him about taking Matt on a paranormal investigation with Dan's group."

"Well, I know he's always been interested in things like that, but I didn't know that he was interested to that extent. I think it's a great idea for him to go with Dan on a paranormal investigation; then he'll know if he really wants to do something like that."

"Looks like we're starting to fill up, so it's time for me to go to work. Why don't you go and mingle while I'm doing the readings? Toni will let you know to come and get me when it's time for Dan to open his presents." She gave him a lingering kiss, then sat down to wait for her first customer.

Nick took his drink and went back inside to grab a quick bite and see if he could find his brother and Brittany. Scanning the crowd, he saw his brother and Brittany engaged in conversation with Henry Bradshaw and his wife. He headed over to join in the conversation. When he arrived, he found them discussing the concept of life after death. Everyone was deep in conversation when suddenly Henry paused in mid-sentence.

"Well, I'll be damned. She's got a lot of nerve to show up here."

"Who are you talking about?" his wife, Diana, asked him.

"What? Oh, I'm sorry, honey, I don't think I told you what happened. About a week ago, I got a visit from Pamela Benson. She wanted me to retract the offer I made to Nick for the new project we're going to start."

"What in the world gives her the right to stick her nose in your business? And what reason did she give you for wanting you to resend your offer?"

"She told me that she had it on good authority that Nick's company was on the brink of bankruptcy because of mismanagement. I pressed her further to find out where she got the information, but she wouldn't say. I knew it was an out and out lie, because I always check into companies before I offer them a project. And I knew that Nick's company was strong. I told her to mind her own business and that if I ever caught her spreading any more of these rumors, I would be talking to Catherine about it."

Nick could feel the anger rising inside of him. He had no idea she could be so vindictive. He knew she had a temper, but he never thought that she would go so far as to try to ruin him.

"You must have done something to really piss her off, and with a woman like that, it could only be one thing. You must have dumped her for another woman," Diana told him.

"Yes, I'm afraid I'm guilty of dumping her, but not for the reason you suggest. I ended our relationship because she was becoming too possessive and was going around telling people we were engaged. Besides, my dog Max never liked her anyway, and he is a great judge of character." Everyone laughed.

"Obviously, she must've come with Catherine. I know for a fact that Toni would never invite her," Brittany chimed in.

"Well, I can almost guarantee that she's up to no good, or she wouldn't be here. And from what you've told me, Nick, she is jealous as hell of Sophie," Matt said, frowning.

"Matt, I need you to take me over to Toni. I need to talk to her about all this," Brittany told him. "Don't worry about it, Nick, we'll take care of it."

"Brittany, you needn't bother Toni. I'll go directly to the source, Catherine. I'm sure she doesn't know what Pamela's been up to, but I think it's time she knew," Diana told them and headed off to where Catherine was holding court across the room.

Sophie had just finished her second reading when she looked up to see Pamela standing in the door of the tent. She could feel the waves of anger and hate emanating from her.

"Hello, Pamela, would you like a reading?" Sophie asked.

"You bitch, you're going to pay for taking Nick away from me. He'll never marry you, you're just a two-bit, phony psychic. When he marries, it will be someone like me, with breeding and culture. He'll come back to me, he always does."

"Are you quite through? He'll never go back to you; you try to control and manipulate him. As for breeding, you come in here screeching like a fishwife, I don't think that's very classy. Why don't you find someone who will let you lead him around by the nose?"

"Why, you little whore, I'll ruin him and you both."

"Tell her you know what she tried to do with Henry and that it didn't work," she heard Martha tell her telepathically. "And let her know that Catherine now knows what she tried to do and she's not happy! Be careful, I don't trust this woman, and neither do Nick's guides."

"I don't think you're going to do anything; you already tried to interfere in Nick's business with Henry, and it didn't work. Now your aunt knows what you tried to do, and I'm sure she's not happy."

She could feel Pamela's anger rising with every word she said. Suddenly, Pamela lunged towards her, hitting her full on in the chest, knocking her through the back of the tent. Sophie tried to catch herself but was unable to stop herself from falling over the edge of the deck. Her last conscious thought was that she hoped this wouldn't ruin Dan's party.

"Bree, you need to get Nick; Sophie's hurt," Martha told her.

"Sophie!" Brittany said out loud.

"Bree, what is it?" Matt asked anxiously.

"Something's happened to Sophie. Her guides are telling me she's hurt. We need to find Nick."

They looked around and saw him sitting at the end of the bar. As they made their way to where he sat, they heard a door slam and looked over in time to see Pamela leaving the building. Bree suspected that she had something to do with what had happened to Sophie.

"Nick, we need to find Sophie. I think she's in trouble."

"She was in her tent when I left her about 30 minutes ago. What makes you think something's happened to her?"

"Martha, one of her guides, came to me and told me she was hurt," Bree told him hurriedly.

Getting up from the bar stool, Nick headed towards the outside patio area, Matt and Bree following behind him.

Making a bee line for Sophie's tent, he looked inside. Her things were scattered all over the floor, and her chair was tipped over, but she was nowhere in sight.

Coming back out of the tent, he surveyed the outside area but couldn't see her anywhere.

"Matt, you two go inside and see if you can find her in there. Bree, make sure you check the bathroom."

"All right, Nick, I wanted to let you know I did see Pamela leave right before Bree got the message from Sophie's guides," Matt told him.

"I think she might have something to do with whatever happened to Sophie; it's just a feeling. But she certainly left in a hurry," Bree told Nick. She and Matt headed into the building to search for her.

Nick headed for the pet area, but she wasn't there and JT was raising a fuss. That gave him an idea. He opened the gate and let JT out. Max started to come out of the gate with JT, but he told him no. "You stay there, Max. JT, where's Sophie? Find Sophie, boy."

JT raised his nose in the air for a moment, sniffing heavily, then headed in the direction of Sophie's tent. He entered the tent, sniffing behind the overturned chair. Picking up and cocking his head to the side, he suddenly pushed through the back of the tent, Nick following closely behind him. JT jumped over the side of the deck, whining at something he had found. Looking over the side of the deck, he saw Sophie lying on the ground. Calling her name, he got no response. Climbing down off the deck, he squatted down beside her body, looking for any signs of injury. He noticed the rise and fall of her chest, so he knew she was alive.

It was then he noticed the blood on a large rock next to Sophie's head. Running his hand around the back of her head, he encountered what felt like a wet, gooey substance. Pulling his hand back, he found it covered in blood. She was unresponsive, and he was afraid to move her. JT whined anxiously and licked Sophie's face.

Pulling out his cell phone, he called 911 and gave their location. He knew it would take a few minutes for the ambulance to get to them. He didn't like the fact that she was unresponsive; he knew she must have hit her head on the stone when she fell.

Dialing Matt's number, he told him what had happened and that an ambulance was on its way. He asked him to let Dan and Toni know what was going on. He told him to watch for the ambulance and guide them to where Nick was waiting. Hanging up, he held

Sophie's hand and spoke to her while trying to calm JT.

The ambulance soon arrived, and they made short work of checking Sophie for broken bones and vital signs. "We're going to take her to Willamette Falls Hospital, you can meet her in the emergency room."

As the ambulance pulled away, Nick headed inside to speak with Toni and Dan. "I'm going to head for the hospital. Can you take JT to your house when the party is over? You'll need to take Sophie's things, too."

"Of course, not to worry; we'll take care of everything. Let me give you our cell and home phone numbers. Call us when you find out more," Toni said, giving Nick their numbers.

"Nick, Bree and I are going with you to the hospital. Bree wants to be there for her when she wakes up," Matt told him.

Saying their goodbyes to Henry and Diana, they headed out the door. Stopping to pick up Zeus, Nick placed JT in the pet care area. They headed for Nick's car and put the dog in the back. "How is Mom going to get home?" Matt wanted to know.

"Henry and Diana told me they would see to it that she and Max got home," Nick told him. Looking up the address for the hospital on his car's GPS, he plotted the quickest course.

Arriving at the hospital, they were told that the doctor was with Sophie and they would be informed when he was done with his exam.

They took a seat in the waiting room and spent the next half-hour waiting for word. To Nick, the wait felt like forever. Suddenly, the door opened and a doctor asked for anyone who was waiting for Sophie.

"Who are you to her?" he asked.

"I'm her fiancé," Nick told him, sensing there was more truth in it than lie. "This is her best friend, her aunt will be down later."

"She has not regained consciousness yet. The MRI shows a fracture of the skull's occipital bone. It's a very minor fracture. Usually, people will regain consciousness shortly after the injury. The brain scan is showing some unusual activity," he said, his expression puzzled.

"That may be associated with her abilities as a psychic medium. I've done some research on the subject," Bree told him.

"Well, we're going to keep her until she regains consciousness. You can come back and see her," he said, opening the door to the back room.

He led them back to a small room where Sophie lay. She looked small, pale and fragile. His heart sank at the sight of her, and he knew in that moment he couldn't live his life without her.

"Matt, can you take me to her?" Bree asked. "I need to touch her to make contact."

Matt helped her avoid the machines and cords to make it to Sophie's side. Taking Sophie's hand in hers, she focused on making contact with her consciousness.

Nick watched Brittany close her eyes, watching emotions flit across her face. Finally, Bree opened her eyes, a look of concern on her face. "I can't make contact with her soul consciousness. That means her consciousness isn't grounded in the body at this moment. We need to bring her consciousness back to her body. Nick, try talking to her, you may be able to draw her back."

"What happens if we can't get her soul consciousness back into her body?" Nick asked.

"If we can't get her consciousness back into her body, the body will eventually die."

Just then, the nurse came in and announced that they were taking Sophie up to a room for overnight observation.

He knew he needed to bring her back, and whatever it took, he was going to do just that. "Matt, you take my car and take Bree and Zeus home, and I'll give you a call to let you know if things change here," he said, handing Matt his car keys.

They left, and Nick followed the gurney up to the room. Once they got her settled and had left, he pulled up the only chair in the room and sat by the bed, holding her hand.

On the astral plane of existence, her guides were attempting to get Sophie to return to her body.

"It's so beautiful here, how can anyone bear to leave this?" Sophie told Martha.

"I know what you mean, but you're not meant to be here, Sophie; it's not your time."

"But I've never felt such unconditional love, except from JT."

"What about JT? Do you want to leave him all alone? You know how much you mean to him. Don't you want to be there for him?" Ann asked.

"I do love him very much, but Toni will take good care of him," she said, smiling.

"What about Nick? I know you love him," Martha said quietly.

"I do love him, but he doesn't love me," she said, shaking her head sadly.

"But he does love you, and I can prove it!" Ann said, grabbing Sophie by the arm.

"Where are we going?"

"I'm taking you to Nick!"

A moment later, they were standing by her body in the hospital room. She could see Nick holding her hand and speaking earnestly to her.

"Sophie, come back to me. I love you so much that life wouldn't be worth living without you. I need you to make me complete. If you don't love me, I'll understand, but I'll keep trying to make you love me. Think of JT and Max; they need you, they love you as much as I do."

Turning her head to look at Ann and Martha, she had a big smile on her face. "He loves me, he really does."

"You had better get back in your body where you belong," Martha said, smiling. "All you have to do is think yourself into your body, and you'll be there."

She must have looked doubtful, because Ann told her, "Over here, it is all about thought; thought becomes reality, so all you have to do is think about it, and it will happen," she reassured her.

"Okay, here goes." Suddenly, she was back in her body, and boy, did she have a terrible headache. She could hear Nick talking, then he paused and asked her a question.

"Sophie, will you marry me?" he asked, his eyes glued to her face for any response.

She could feel herself smiling, and her eyes fluttered open. "Yes, I'll marry you, I love you with all my heart."

Nick let out a cry of pure joy and lifted her into his arms. It was only when he tried to cradle her head that she let out a cry of pain. He was immediately contrite. "I'm sorry, sweetheart, I didn't mean to hurt you," he said, gently placing her back in the bed.

"That's okay, I must have hit my head when Pamela pushed me off the deck," she said, trying to put the pieces together. She noticed the anger in his eyes when she mentioned what had happened.

"That woman has a lot to answer for, and I'll make sure she does!" he said with a grim look on his face.

She reached up and stroked his face. "She's not worth the effort. After all, if she hadn't pushed me off the deck, I might not have known that you loved me."

He reached down and gently kissed her mouth. "I would have figured it out sooner or later and done something about it," he told her, grinning. "One thing you'll have to learn about me is, I may be stubborn and hardheaded, but I'm not stupid. I know when I have a good thing, even though it may take me a while to realize it. I'd better call everyone to let them know you're okay."

"Do you think they'll let me go home tonight?"

"I certainly hope so, I want you all to myself. I promise to take good care of you! I'm going to find someone who can release you." With that, he headed out the door to the nurses' station. A few minutes later, he came back with the doctor in tow.

By the time the hospital released her, it was 8 o'clock. Nick dialed Matt's cell phone number and asked him to swing by Toni's to pick up JT, then come and pick them up. Forty-five minutes later, they were just heading out the door of the hospital as Matt pulled the car up.

JT could be heard whining loudly once he saw Sophie. "It's all right, big man, you can sit in the back with Matt while we head home."

The trip to Sophie's house seemed to take forever; Nick was driving slower, so as not to jar Sophie's head. Pulling into the driveway, he noticed that someone had brought Sophie's SUV home for her. Matt got the house keys from Sophie's purse, and Nick carried her inside and up into her living quarters, with JT and Matt following closely behind. Placing her on the sofa, he turned and spoke to Matt.

"You go ahead and take my car, you can bring it back in the morning. I'm staying to take care of her tonight."

"Okay, I'll give you a call before I head over in the morning." Matt had to keep himself from smiling. He had never seen his big brother act like this with any woman before. It had to be love. Whether he was willing to admit it or not was an altogether different matter. Wait until he told Mom about this, she would be over the moon. Getting the car, he headed over to his mom's house to let her know what was going on.

"It's about time that son of mine wised up and found a good woman. It's even better that she can hear me when I need to give him some advice," Bill said, grinning at the other guides.

"He seems to be doing fine in regards to the business, and now that he and Sophie are together, things will be better all around," Helen commented.

"Ain't love grand?" Sid injected with a sappy grin on his face.

"Let's leave them alone for a while, shall we?" Martha said. She motioned for them to head for the roof, and they followed. They spent the next several hours catching up on all the latest news.

Sitting down beside her on the couch, Nick asked, "Do you want anything? I could get us something to eat."

He appeared so anxious to do something for her that she took pity on him. "There are lunch meats and cheese in the refrigerator. The bread is in the bread box on the counter. If you could do me a favor and feed JT. There's a large container in the fridge; take some out of it and warm it in the microwave for about a minute. His bowl is on the floor, next to his water dish."

"Of course, he must be starving. You didn't have anything either. I'll fix us a couple of sandwiches." Heading for the kitchen, he heard her say, "There's a bowl of fruit salad in the fridge we can have with it."

Opening the fridge, he found JT's food and put it in to warm while he got out the sandwich meats. A thought just occurred to him, he headed for the kitchen doorway and asked, "Do you want mayo or mustard or both?"

She smiled at him and said, "Lightly on both, please, and there's some lettuce and tomatoes in the crisper. I'm afraid I don't have anything but milk, coffee and water to offer you."

"No problem, I'll survive with water," he said, smiling at her. The microwave beeped, and he spooned JT's food into his bowl and set it on the floor.

He soon made short work of preparing the sandwiches and fruit salad. Carrying a plate in for both of them, he set it on the coffee table and headed back to the kitchen for the spoons and water. They ate in silence, relishing the food and just being together.

"When did you first know you loved me?" she asked him.

He thought for a moment. "I think I knew when I first looked up into your eyes. In that moment, I fell for you in more ways than one. I didn't want to admit it, I fought against it. I thought it was just a physical attraction, I even went so far as to have sex with Pamela to try to get you out of my system. Needless to say, it didn't work; it only made me realize how much I had come to dislike her and everything she stood for. It was only when I saw you lying motionless on the ground and I thought you were dead that I admitted it to myself."

She could tell it was hard for him to admit these things to her. She wasn't even jealous of Pamela; she could almost pity her. "When we first met, I was leery because I sensed you were a diehard skeptic. I had been hurt before when I was younger. He was tall, good looking and from a very proper family. He wanted someone he and his family could mold into the perfect wife. I thought we were in love, but he was only infatuated with his own image of what he wanted me to be. I did try to fit in at first, I changed my clothes, hair, makeup and went to all the right parties. I soon learned that I was only in love with love. When I told him about my abilities, he looked at me like I was a freak. He told me that if we were going to get married, I would have to give up 'all that nonsense', as he put it. It was then that I knew with absolute certainty that he was not the one for me. I swore then and there that if I ever met a man I was in love with, I would make certain he knew what I was about. He would have to accept me for what I am, and not what they want me to be!"

"Honey, I'm sorry you were hurt, but his loss is my good fortune," he said, grinning at her and kissing her long and hard.

When she could catch her breath, she told him, "That's why I was always leery about dating anyone. I had to be sure that anyone I got involved with would accept me for myself."

"I love every bit of you. I may not always understand what you do, but I will support you in anything you do," he promised her. "Now, when will you marry me?"

She smiled secretively at him, stood up, took his hand and headed for the bedroom. "Let's discuss this later," she said.

He smiled back and picked her up and carried her to the bedroom, placing her gently on the bed.

A soft whine sounded just inside the door. Turning to look, they saw JT standing at the entrance to the room. Smiling at the dog, she reassured him that she was fine and that he needed to go to his bed, not share hers tonight. He seemed to grin, then turned and headed out of the room.

"What was that all about?" Nick asked.

"He was confused. He wanted to sleep with me like he usually does, but I told him he couldn't tonight because you were here. He's never seen anyone in my bed but me, so he was unsure where he fit in. I told him I would talk to him about it tomorrow, and I told him I loved him. That seemed to reassure him."

"Should I shut the door?"

"You can if it makes you feel more comfortable, but he won't come into the room tonight unless we ask him to."

"I'll shut it anyway so we won't keep him awake," Nick told her, but her knowing grin told him she knew he felt uncomfortable leaving it open.

He closed the door, then stood by the bed and removed his clothes.

Sophie watched as he removed his clothes without self-consciousness. His body was lean, muscular and chiseled without being gross. She sat up and started to remove her clothes, but he stopped her.

"Let me do that for you, I want to get to know every part of you, inside and out," he said, running his lips over her body as he removed her clothes.

His lips and hands brought her senses and body to life in places where no other man had ever touched. By the time her clothes had been removed, every part of her body was on fire. As he entered her, he felt resistance and pulled back. "Sophie?"

She saw the question in his eyes. "I have never felt this way with any other man, you're the first."

"That ex-fiancé of yours was more of an idiot than I thought. Are you all right with this?" he asked.

Seeing her nod her head, he spoke softly, "I promise I'll be gentle."

Entering her slowly, he felt her body tense with pain, then relax. He took his time to build her pleasure to the point that matched his own need for her, then there was no holding back for either of them as they climaxed together. Afterward, they lay entwined, tired and complete.

She could feel him still nestled inside of her, and she liked how it made her feel, whole, complete.

Nick had never felt this way before; it was as if she completed him. All the sexual encounters that he had experienced before were merely sex; this was lovemaking. He wasn't sure where he ended and she began. "I love you, Sophie, and I want to have many children with you."

"Wow, how many are we talking about? Personally, I would settle for 2 or 3," she said, grinning up at him.

"How about a half-dozen? But it's negotiable." He grinned back at her.

"How about we keep it at 3 and have 6 dogs instead?" she asked.

"Done, let's get started."

She could feel him stirring inside her, and that was her last coherent thought for the rest of the night.

Outside on the front porch, two sets of guides were congratulating each other on a job well done.

"Well, I'm so glad we finally got them together," Martha said.

"I thought for a while there that Nick would never admit his feelings for Sophie. I'm glad we were able to give Sophie a little shove in the right direction, with a little help from Pamela," Bert agreed.

Sid, Helen and Ann looked at each other as suspicion dawned.

"Are you trying to tell me you two interfered in their lives?" Helen asked.

""What about this whole non-interference thing, or does it only pertain to guides in training?" Ann wanted to know.

"Yeah, governor, what about the free will you're always going on about?" Sid asked, his accent more pronounced in his agitation.

"All right, all right, we freely admit to interfering in their lives, but sometimes you have to give them a swift kick in the other end to get them going in the right direction," Bert said.

"We knew that eventually they would get together, we were just helping it along a bit. It's not like we changed the outcome; just moved the timeline up a bit," Martha told them.

The three younger guides gave the two older ones a knowing look.

"Please tell me you didn't influence Pamela to push Sophie off the deck?" Ann asked Martha.

"Sometimes drastic measures are needed to set things in motion, and no, I didn't do it; I had her guides do it," Martha said with a slight smile.

Sid grinned at Ann. "Told you they were up to something. That's why Pamela's guides wouldn't talk to me, I'll bet."

"Well, the least you could have done was let us in on your plan," Helen said, sulking.

"Cheer up, Helen, I promise to give you a heads up next time I do anything underhanded," Bert told, her smiling.

They all laughed and began to talk about the future and the children that were yet to come.

Epilogue
Fifteen months later

"I just can't get over how beautiful our son is." Nick said holding his 2 month old son, Dominic.

"He has your coloring but my eyes, he's definitely going to be a lady killer." Sophie agreed. The combination of black hair, olive complexion and topaz eyes was enough to stop any woman in her tracks. Add in empathic abilities and you have an irresistible package. When the time was right they would have to have a serious discussion about how to treat women.

"Nick you had better put Dom down and get ready, your Mom will be here in a few minutes." She said smiling not for the first time at his fascination with his son.

"Alright." Sitting him down in his swing Nick headed for the bedroom to finish dressing.

JT and Max made a beeline for the baby and sat down one on either side of the swing as if guarding him. Sophie watched as the baby looked at each dog in turn. Each dog licked him gently on the cheek.

"He has several of your abilities you know" Martha told her.

"Yes his abilities will be stronger than yours. You'll need to have a firm hand with him growing up or there will be more than one broken heart." Bert agreed.

"Have you told him yet?" Ann wanted to know.

"No, I haven't told him yet but I will tonight."

"What are you waiting for? There's no time like the present." Helen interjected.

"I suppose you're right, although I hadn't planned on having another baby quite so soon." Sophie said.

"Not to worry love, this one will be another charmer but a girl this time." Sid told her.

"I know, which means he'll be even more protective then he is already." Sophie said.

The doorbell rang and her mother-in-law walked into the house. Heading straight for the baby she scooped him up and twirled around making the baby giggle.

"You're going to spoil him, you know." Sophie told her laughing.

"Of course I am, isn't that what grandma's are for?"

"Yes you're absolutely right about that."

"Have you told Nick yet?" Jewel asked Sophie.

Sophie should have guessed that Jewel would have already figured out her secret.

"Told Nick what?" Nick asked walking into the room. Looking at both of their guilty faces he grew more curious. "Sophie?"

"Nick, I want you to sit down for a minute." Nick sat down not sure what was coming.

"Nick darling, you're going to be a father again in about 8 months."

He sat there with a look of stunned surprise on his face. "Darling, you are happy about it aren't you?" she asked worriedly.

A huge smile lit his face, "Happy? I'm over the moon, I can hardly wait to tell Matt. He'll be so happy to be an uncle again. Do we know if it will be another boy or a girl?"

She gave him a mischievous smile, "Its going to be a little girl."

"Well if she's anything like her mother I'm going to have my hands full beating off the guys."

They all laughed in delight at the thought of two pint sized mischief makers running around the house.

"Should we tell them about the third child?" Bert wanted to know.

"No, I think one surprise is enough for today, besides the third child is going to be no less special, but in a different way. Let them have their peace and quiet for now." Martha told him and they both grinned in anticipation of what was to come.